W9-AHY-880

AND ALL OUR WOUNDS FORGIVEN

Also by Julius Lester:

Look Out, Whitey! Black Power's Gon' Get Your Mama
To Be a Slave
Revolutionary Notes
Black Folktales
Search for the New Land
The Seventh Son: The Thought and Writings of W.E.B.
Du Bois
Long Journey Home: Stories from Black History
Two Love Stories
The Knee-High Man
Who I Am (with David Gahr)
All Is Well
This Strange New Feeling
Do Lord Remember Me
The Tales of Uncle Remus: The Adventures of Brer Rabbit
More Tales of Uncle Remus: Further Adventures of Brer
Rabbit
Further Tales of Uncle Remus
The Last Tales of Uncle Remus
Lovesong: Becoming a Jew
How Many Spots Does a Leopard Have?
Falling Pieces of the Broken Sky

AND ALL OUR WOUNDS FORGIVEN

Julius Lester

Arcade Publishing • New York

FIRST EDITION

This is a work of fiction. Names, characters, places and incidents are either the product of the author's imagination or used fictitiously.

Library of Congress Cataloging-in-Publication Data

Lester, Julius.
    And all our wounds forgiven / Julius Lester.
        p. cm.
    ISBN 1-55970-258-3
    1. Civil rights workers — United States — Fiction.   2. Afro-American men — Fiction.   I. Title.
    PS3562.E853A83   1994
    813'.54 — dc20   93-50049

Published in the United States by Arcade Publishing, Inc., New York
Distributed by Little, Brown and Company

10 9 8 7 6 5 4 3 2 1

BP

Designed by API

PRINTED IN THE UNITED STATES OF AMERICA

To
Milan Sabatini
evermore

AND ALL OUR WOUNDS
FORGIVEN

i do not know where the story begins. though i am integral to it, i am not sure i know even what the story is as neither my life nor death constitutes *the* story.

nor is the story always the one we recall. rarely is it the one we tell.

in its etymological root, *story* means to see. hi-story is, then, the record of what was seen. there's the rub, to coin a phrase. what constitutes seeing? is such profundity even possible? *who* is seeing determines what is seen. can we hope, then, for more than awareness of what we *think* we see, though what we see may not be there at all?

example: in the mid-fifties i *saw* that the time had come to end racial segregation in the south. the 1954 supreme court decision outlawing racial segregation in public schools was like a second emancipation proclamation for us. the highest court in the land was, at long last, ready to uphold the constitutional principle of equality under the law. by decree-ing segregation in public schools unconstitutional, the court, wittingly or unwittingly, had declared segregation illegal in every aspect of american life.

i was under no illusion that ending segregation on buses, in restaurants and in other areas of public accommodation would be easy. i and others would give our lives. dying for the right to sit on a torn seat at the front of a bus was not an even exchange. but such obscene inequity was inherent to the story. i thought that was all i needed to understand.

how little i knew about the nature of *story*. i still believed stories had the calming order of beginnings, middles and ends, with unambiguous heroes, heroines and villains. if i acted for the good, the good would prevail and justice would roll through the land with the meandering majesty of a mighty river.

what gave me such confidence to think i knew what the good was? i equated recognition of injustice with apprehension of the good. such elegant symmetry is only in the minds of political ideologues. whatever judgement history makes of my life, it will not record that john calvin marshall was an ideologue.

yet, i, too, was guilty of oversimplifying, of trying to contain the story within the parameters of my subjective landscape. i believed that if you sincerely and honestly acted for the good, goodness would be the consequence.

how little i knew.

once set in motion, social change, regardless of its noble intent and pure righteousness, cannot be controlled. you think you are changing "this" and you are. but you did not anticipate "that" changing also. by the time recognition of the unanticipated consequences comes, it is too late to do anything — except hope you survive.

i thought social change meant the enactment of laws to modify behavior and eliminate or at least reform institutions that acted unjustly and punish those who refused to alter their behavior, if not their attitudes.

i learned:

social change is the transformation of values by which a group and/or nation has defined and known itself. such change is like pregnancy; a woman is aware of it only a month after conception. a nation becomes cognizant of a shift in its values only when facing a phenomenon it does not understand and can find no precedent for.

example: 1956: i was 26 years old, a harvard ph.d. andrea and i had been married for a year. congress authorized the construction of an interstate highway system. i'm sure we read about it in the paper. i have no doubt that huntley-brinkley mentioned it one evening in their droll, offhand way that made cynicism not only acceptable but attractive. there was probably a picture in the atlanta constitution of president eisenhower in the rose garden or oval office using thirty pens to sign the bill into law. we did not pay attention because we thought it was a wonderful idea. we remembered the drive from boston to atlanta the year before. part of the new jersey turnpike had been built by then and what a treat it was to drive at 65 miles an hour for unbroken stretches. but most of that journey was made on two lane highways through small southern towns where the speed limit was 35 and, if you were colored, you got arrested for doing 34. i greeted the projected interstate highway system with anticipation. that i did so indicated a transmutation of my values of which i was as yet unaware.

like all other americans in the fifties, i had become a believer in the ethic of saving time. (bear with me if i appear to be rambling. i am not. for some the exercise of logic means moving straight ahead. on this side of the veil, we tend to go sideways but are no less logical.)

saving time is a peculiar concept. what does it mean? and how do you do it?

theoretically, you reduce the time used for one task and free time for other activities. sounds reasonable. but is it? shake-speare "wasted" a lot of time because he wrote in long hand with quill pens. it would be logical to conclude that if he had had a ballpoint pen, typewriter or computer, he would have written more plays and perhaps, greater ones. yet, no user of a ballpoint pen, typewriter or computer has equaled or excelled him in applying the english language to human experience. it is possible shakespeare would have written less and less well had he used a computer.

perhaps shakespeare neither spent or saved time but lived in different relationship to it. perhaps he wore time. perhaps it wore him.

the twentieth-century metaphor for our relationship to time implies ownership. "how much time do we have?" is a common question. "i wasted a lot of time sitting in traffic," is a daily plaint. "i have some free time tomorrow afternoon." we conceive of time as a commodity to be expended, hoarded or wasted. the marxist — when such existed — would have said the metaphor reflects capitalism. it is not so simple.

the interstate highway system was created to save time. how much time? if two cars leave new york city for albany at noon, one driving 65, the other 55, the first car will arrive twelve minutes before the second. i suppose if you had to go to the bathroom badly, knocking twelve minutes off a three hour drive would be helpful. otherwise, what would one do with the twelve minutes saved?

but what one does with the time saved is not the issue. an american axiom: better to have wasted the time you've saved than not to have saved it at all. some are so conscientious about saving time they drive 80 and 90 miles an hour and save themselves the most time of all — the rest of their lives.

what was not anticipated was the enormous social change the interstate highway system would bring into being. for centuries we had been rooted to place. home and work and leisure occurred in one place and created a whole — community. the interstate highway system made it possible to live thirty, forty, fifty, sixty miles from where you worked. work and home and place ceased to be interrelated. you could work in a city whose people and institutions were alien to you. you could live in a place and be indifferent to its people and institutions. you could live and be unknown at work and at home. You could live without belonging to a community. (enter the nuclear family as locus of society. but the family is too small an entity to withstand the intricate permutations of relationship. the pressures of family are alleviated only if the family knows itself as part of a community. when it does not, we should not be surprised that one out of two marriages end in divorce.)

the interstate highway system brought into being a geopolitical entity called sub-urbs as people discovered they could have the amenities of country living on city incomes.

eventually, stores and corporations moved to where their workers and consumers had gone. the middle-class white collar workforce and corporations that had provided the tax base for the urbs took their tax dollars to the sub-urbs. the cities deteriorated because the majority of the inhabitants remaining were blacks, hispanics and poor whites who did not have incomes to generate sufficient tax revenues. america became a nation of predominantly white sub-urbs encircling black and poor urbs. why? is it too harsh to conclude that we cared more about saving time than about the structure of our society?

saving time became a national priority. the fifties saw the introduction of ballpoint pens, minute rice, tv dinners and fast food restaurants — mcdonald's, kentucky fried chicken and pizza hut. why did we become obsessed with *saving* what cannot be saved?

world war ii. it taught us that we could die — not individually, each in his and her own time, but all at once, together, with no one left to remember who we had been, or even that we had been.

truman said he slept peacefully after he made the decision to drop the atomic bombs on hiroshima and nagasaki, that he never had a second thought because the decision shortened the war and saved american lives. that is good. but it is a good encompassing so little. we see only the magic circle we draw around us and ours, and by definition, whatever protects us and ours is the intrinsic good. we remain oblivious to the intrinsic evil snoring quietly on the other side of the circle.

truman's limited good changed the fundamental definition of how we lived on the planet. i was 15 when the bombs were dropped. a profound difference between me and those young people who gathered around me in the civil rights movement was they grew up knowing sentient existence on the planet could be destroyed by human volition. they grew up numbed by the second world war, which deliberately, willfully, knowingly made civilians the objects of mass destruction. dresden, auschwitz, hiroshima, nagasaki. 54,800,000 people, mostly civilians, died in world war ii. the object of war was no longer territory; the object of war became death. how could anyone born after 1946 trust life?

being born in 1930 i grew up in a world in which the continuity of life was unquestioned. after hiroshima and auschwitz i could not trust life naively anymore, but neither did I distrust it. instead, my generation was infected by a virus called existential anxiety. we were not comfortable with life or death and lived in fear of both.

those born after hiroshima were beyond anxiety. anxiety implies that life can be trusted if you learn how to relate to it. the post-hiroshima citizen trusts only death, because it is the singular and ultimate security, the one experience that can be depended on to be what it claims to be. those of us whose consciousness predates hiroshima retain an ancestral memory of the nobility of the human experiment. our angst is leavened by faith in the dignity of the human being. when faulkner stood at stockholm in 1949 and declared "man will prevail," he affirmed the secular catechism that had held the west together since the renaissance. then he went and had a bourbon-and-branch.

that first generation of post-hiroshima youth loved me, for a while, because they longed for this secular faith.

however, during the last days of my life, i saw them swallowed alive by the idolization of race. blacks placed racial exaltation above a love of humanity and did not understand: their love of race was passion for death, a passion ignited in the extermination camps, and at hiroshima and nagasaki.

when civilians became the targets of government weaponry, whatever semblance of safety government represented was destroyed. it did not matter that it was our government against someone else's. truman miscalculated the extent to which people were willing to go to save american lives. we saw photographs of the mushroom clouds in life magazine and read the stories of women and children vaporized from the face of the earth, leaving behind only their shadows burned into the ground. no shots were fired on american soil in ww ii. no bombs fell on american cities. yet, americans seemed to understand inchoately that murder carried to its logical extreme is self-murder. when the soviet union acquired a nuclear capability, it became clear: governments were now willing to destroy the world to save the nation.

after auschwitz, after hiroshima, saving time became an obsession because we could no longer assume that the human experiment on planet earth would continue until its natural end was reached hundreds of millions of years later when the sun's heat consumes the planet. our descendants were no longer guaranteed to us. we were compelled to *save time* because at auschwitz and at hiroshima, time was destroyed.

we mistake for the Good the limited good we see — or think we see — or rationalize that we see — or lie about. we do not want to see that what is good today may spawn evil tomorrow. evil is not an absolute. evil is ambiguous, and sometimes, it does not seek to negate the good but merely hold its hand. for many of us, this is worse. good that is ashamed of itself loses its vitality. it should not. good and evil are not distinct. they interpenetrate each other continually until it is unclear which is which. if one is patient, you eventually understand that it does not matter. good or evil are merely opinions we offer based on notions of what is convenient and inconvenient to us, our group, our nation.

and if i had known . . .

LISA

A tall woman, straight blond hair brushing her shoulders, sat by the bed of a comatose black woman in a Nashville, Tennessee, hospital.

The white woman had appeared early that afternoon. Shyly, almost fearfully, she asked if she could see Andrea Marshall. If not for the offering of respect in her voice, the head nurse, an almost equally tall black woman, would have assumed she was a reporter. She was about to tell her someone was in the room already, the man who had come in the ambulance with Mrs. Marshall last night, when, from the far end of the corridor, she saw him coming toward them. As he got closer he looked up, saw the white woman at the nurse's station, stopped, and said, "Lisa?"

"Bobby?"

They embraced with the overeagerness of two who had been absent from each other more years than had been shared. Yet, the looks they exchanged (once past the comparing of hairlines (his) and gray strands (hers)) were a tentative affirmation of the memories joining them, memories as defining of their lives as if they had been married and buried their only child. They embraced again with a tremor of anxiety at this unexpected resurrection of a past that, apparently, had not been buried and now appeared not even to have died, and, unlike them, had not aged.

They released each other and stepped back. "You look as trim and fit as ever," he commented, admiringly. She nodded. "I stay in shape." She couldn't help but note that he had not. It had been — what? — almost thirty years since she had sneaked him out of Shiloh in the middle of the night and taken him to New York (for reasons she was never told). That man had been thin, almost emaciated. This one was rounded, like a balloon blown up slowly, care being taken to cut off the air before the wisp that would pop the skin. He had become a sphere of a man, the dome of his bald head atop an even rounder body supported by legs that appeared too thin for the weight imposed upon them.

"It's good to see you." The earnestness in his voice would have made her blush if it had come from an adolescent boy. But he was not a teenager and there was a bewilderment in his eyes, not at the present moment that had brought them together but about life itself. There was something he had failed to grasp, and sooner than he would have thought, a half-century of living was past tense and more sentences began with "I remember when . . ." than with "I am going to . . ." and he was alone, a pain in his heart like the aching of milk in a woman's breasts as the tiny coffin of her child was placed tenderly in the grave. Such loneliness lacked even the illusory edge of a horizon. Elizabeth preferred gazing into the night sky when she wanted to contemplate infinity.

"How long are you staying?"

She shook her head. "I don't know."

"Well, I hope long enough for us to have a chance to talk."

"That would be good," came the unanticipated response, and hearing it, she felt poised on a crest of unshed and unwanted tears. "How's Andrea?" she asked quickly.

"She hasn't regained consciousness, and the doctors don't know if or when."

"Had she been ill?"

He shook his head. "No. I took her to church yesterday and she was fine. We spent the afternoon editing her diaries for publication, and, around eight, just as I was getting ready to go, she collapsed. I called the ambulance and I've been here every since."

Diaries! Andrea had kept a diary? Elizabeth looked at Bobby with renewed interest. How much did he know? How much truth was Andrea telling? Had a truth she feared speaking struck with force enough to paralyze her?

"Would it be OK if I sat with her?" she asked, not wanting to cry, not now, not yet, not until she knew for whom or to what she would be yielding.

"That would be great. It would give me the chance to go home, make some calls and get some sleep."

She hadn't moved from her bedside, not even to go to the cafeteria or the bathroom. When passing in the hallway, nurses, especially the black ones, glanced through the open door of the room (it wasn't everyday somebody famous was in the hospital. The White House had called last night!) and would see Elizabeth's lips moving. If her eyes hadn't been open, they might have thought she was praying (though she didn't look like the kind who knew very much about the Lord, not that you could judge a body's soul from a diamond ring on their finger big enough to bowl with, or from the leather coat laid carelessly over the other chair in the room. That coat was a month of paychecks for an R.N., which didn't mean she wasn't as God-fearing as the Pope even if her nails were manicured as precisely as cut diamonds.)

But prayer was not to be confused with church books or the words that came from preachers' mouths with the ease of profanity. Prayer was the painful submission to the colors in a tear and the mystery of a stone, and when she had heard on the eleven o'clock news the night before that "Andrea

Williams Marshall, widow of slain civil rights leader, John Calvin Marshall, suffered a stroke this evening and is listed in grave condition in a Nashville, Tennessee, hospital," she had gotten up immediately, gone to her computer, and through her modem, accessed airline schedules, made a reservation and, before dawn, driven down from the mountain and through the snow in her Blazer. It had taken five hours rather than the usual three to get to Logan Airport in Boston.

Gregory said she didn't think. That was not true. She didn't think as he did. He examined every decision through a round and angled mirror as if it were the tooth of one of his patients. He poked and scraped with the curved hooks of needle-thin instruments, afraid there might be an emotional plaque eating away unseen at the soul.

She acted and explained later, if at all. Nothing made a man feel more unloved than not knowing why. But for her, and she suspected, most women, having to answer a "Why?" was like hitting the brakes on an icy road while doing 60. So she had flown to Nashville, not even telling Gregory where she was going. He would've asked questions for which she didn't have answers. If she had paused and reflected, doubt would have eroded her confidence and left her in stasis — and at home.

For her, knowledge resided in the loins, a certainty like the shifting of the body's center of gravity when her hips and thighs balanced the alternate edges of skis as she essed down a mountain slope on virgin snow. If there were thought at such times, she was *its* object. From the moment she heard the news she had known only that she needed to be with Andrea.

Maybe it was not important if Andrea heard (and would she have come if Andrea could have listened and said in return?). But after thirty years, it was time.

She stared at the woman in the bed, struck yet again at how much younger than her age she had always looked. She was not so much beautiful as handsome. Like many black women she seemed to have gone from youth to agelessness and become an icon of Woman, primordial, eternal, her face a mask holding in perfect equilibrium the cycles of every woman's life.

"You always looked ten years younger than your age, even the first time I saw you. It was here in Nashville, in the chapel at Fisk. April, 1960. The sit-ins had begun and John Calvin Marshall, *the* John Calvin Marshall, had come to speak. I was an exchange student from Pomona College in California, here not even two months and found myself thrust into history like a slice of apple into cheese fondue. Everybody thought I was special because I had sat in and gotten arrested. There weren't many blond, blue-eyed twenty-year-old white girls willing to risk getting beat up by the police or a mob, being called 'nigger lover' and spat on. I was the all-American girl. Ever since I was small, people have looked at me and seen corn fields, amber waves of grain and spacious skies. When I walked into rooms you could almost smell apple pie baking and hear 'The Star-Spangled Banner' in the background. And there I was on a lunch counter stool surrounded by blacks, protesting racial segregation. Blacks loved me and whites wanted to kill me."

She stopped and stared into the distance, a sadness covering her eyes as if she were recalling a love that could have been fulfilled if only ———

❖

may 17 1954. i was working on my dissertation at harvard. i left my carrel at the widener library to go for a walk. i happened to wander to harvard square where i passed a newsstand. there, on the front page the headline — the supreme court had declared segregation in public schools unconstitutional. i bought a copy and ran to andrea's dorm at radcliffe to share the good news, news as revolutionary as the emancipation proclamation.

what did i know? i was a dumb colored boy getting a ph.d in philosophy. i could not have imagined that the south would defy the supreme court. we were a nation of laws, were we not? public officials, from the president to congress to governors and mayors and county sheriffs, took office with their hands on bibles swearing to uphold the law and the constitution. i was to learn otherwise.

conventional wisdom is that the civil rights movement started with the bus boycott i organized in atlanta or the sit-in movement of the students in 1960. that is not so. historians overlook the enormous impact on the consciousness of the negro when we saw governors and mayors and u.s. senators and congressmen actively defying the highest court in the land, aggressively urging white people to resist desegregation. i still remember the cover of an issue of look magazine: the south says never.

philosophically, the issue was framed as states' rights, that is, the states had rights that the federal government could not contravene. but, i argued silently, what happens when affirming states' rights violates the constitution that binds the states into a nation of laws? america was facing a constitutional crisis that, a hundred years before, had led to civil war. this time, however, war was declared on the negro.

across the south the crude violence and terror of the ku klux klan was replaced by the white shirts and ties of middle-class southern business men and leaders who organized the white citizens council. it terrorized negroes in more sophisticated ways. in mississippi the council threatened the job of any negro who looked like he or she wanted to desegregate the schools. the number of registered black voters in the state dropped from 12,000 to 8,000 in less than a year. in georgia, where fate was to send me, the state board of education ordered all teachers who were members of the naacp to resign from the organization or have their teaching licenses revoked. the year following the school decision, the supreme court ruled that segregated public golf courses, parks, swimming pools and playgrounds were unconstitutional. many southern towns closed their public parks, playgrounds and swimming pools.

for me, the final straw came in 1956. i was now DR. john calvin marshall. with my bride of a year i moved to atlanta where i had secured a position at spelman college, the school for black women. i remember the evening we sat in the living room after supper, andrea looking at the newspaper while i went over my notes on plato's *symposium*, wondering how did i teach a treatise on homosexual love to the creme de la creme of negro society?

andrea: have you seen this?

what? i asked.

southern congressmen have issued a manifesto urging the use quote of all lawful means unquote to overturn brown v. board of education.

she read me the names of those who signed the so-called manifesto. they were some of the most prominent in the congress:

strom thurmond of south carolina who race-baited when that would keep him in office and in the seventies learned to say black instead of nigra when that would keep him in office; j.w. fulbright of arkansas, the same fulbright whose name is associated with graduate fellowships for the best and brightest, as in, "i got a fulbright"; i didn't; wilbur d. mills, prominent member of the house who would be arrested for cavorting in a d.c. fountain with a very attractive and very young woman; hale boggs, congressman from louisiana who would die in a plane crash in alaska and one of whose daughters would become a prominent newscaster and political analyst; and sam ervin, the folksy, country lawyer, the principal author of the manifesto, who would become hero of the watergate hearings, which led to the downfall of president nixon. in all 101 senators and congressmen signed. the only ones who did not were lyndon johnson, and the two senators from tennessee, estes kefauver and albert gore, sr.

something broke inside me as andrea and i discussed this ignorant insistence on continuing the cruelty of racial segregation. i had been resolutely denying the evident: the south had no intention of obeying the law of the land. that evening i acceded to the story and i saw: if white senators and white congressmen, white governors and white mayors would so openly and brazenly and willfully disobey the constitution, why couldn't the negro brazenly disobey laws that were unconstitutional. if southern whites broke the law to uphold injustice, the negro had to break the law and uphold justice.

how ironic that in the late sixties president nixon was elected by decrying the breakdown in law and order. white people, northern and southern, saw their cities go up in flame and smoke as summer after summer, blacks took to the streets in blind fury, no more so than after my assassination. the flame and smoke could be seen from the white house. how hypocritical the outrage of white americans at what they considered a criminal disregard for law and order by blacks. law and order had broken down a decade before when southern elected officials encouraged and applauded defiance of the supreme court. the sixties were created by white people who thought their prejudices and bigotry were rights that had precedence over the constitution. their open defiance of the law as well as the refusal by other whites to decry *that* breakdown in law and order were what thrust me into a history i had always feared. what else would have motivated an alabama colored boy to learn greek and find a security in fifth century b.c. athens that he found nowhere in twentieth century america?

andrea and i knew i would be killed eventually and decided we should not have children. to be a widow was one kind of pain. to be an orphan was another entirely, she said. i agreed, but reluctantly. it was a decision i always regretted. by not having children we broke faith with the future. we also broke faith with each other.

around this time i saw a picture of jackie kennedy in the newspaper or a magazine. she was still the wife of the senator from massachusetts then but this was no ordinary politician's wife. she was young and she was beautiful and she was smiling a smile that had confidence in tomorrow. after that i looked for pictures of her in the paper and periodicals. jackie's smile gave me hope the world didn't have to be the way it was, that the world couldn't remain as it was in the face of that smile and confidence in what i didn't know but it gave me confidence too and i don't know if any of what happened in the sixties would have if not for jfk and the kennedy hair blowing in the wind on a sailing boat off nantucket, the spiral of a football in the autumn air on the white house lawn, the easy self-mocking sense of humor (something harvard men do better than anyone) and jackie's smile.

we are taught that history is powered by ideals and men and women of vision and greatness. not at all. what we remember is the jut of fdr's jaw, the uptilt of his cigarette in its holder, the air of command and easy confidence even from a wheelchair. what we remember of jack and bobby are the unruly hair, the free, open and boyish grins, the insouciant shine in the eyes giving them the sheen of eternal youth. camelot it was called because we all felt young and because we did, we partook of immortality and the surety we could do no wrong. it was a dangerous time.

i liked but never trusted either of the kennedy brothers. but we needed their exuberance and playfulness after the shock of the cold war, eisenhower, joe mccarthy.

social change does not occur when people suffer most acutely. totalitarianism works as long as a government has the stomach to impose terror every hour on the hour. a terrorized people can do nothing more than focus their attentions on recognizing and seizing an unguarded moment during the day. the psychological terror of segregation in the south was a totalitarianism that succeeded until jackie's smile and jfk's wit gave us hope that things could be different.

i remember my phone ringing early the evening of february 1, 1960. it was a monday. (in a few years I would look back

with longing to that time when i could answer my own tele-
phone.) it was a colleague from greensboro, north carolina,
telling me that four black students from north carolina had
sat down on lunch-counter stools at a variety store that
afternoon and did not move when they were refused service. they had just been arrested.

(that was no spontaneous act, i learned later. a white professor at the college had been looking for students to challenge segregation by sitting in. Finally, history produced
four.)

my greensboro caller wondered if i would make some calls
to see if demonstrations to support the students could be
organized in a few cities like atlanta and nashville, cities
with a number of negro and white colleges and universities
and therefore prone to be more liberal in their racial attitudes
if not in law.

by the following wednesday, sit-ins were underway in fifteen
cities in five states across the south. let me hasten to add
that i take no credit. when i called a colleague at fisk in
nashville, they were planning sit-ins of their own, an action
that went far beyond a sympathy demonstration.

we think an individual can sit astride hi-story and direct it
to the right or left as if it were a tennessee walking horse.
that is not so. (people talk as if i made the civil rights movement by myself. what did they think they were accomplishing
by making a holiday of my birthday or putting my face on a
stamp? what surer way to rob my life of value, integrity and
meaning than turn me into a monument.)

i did not act as much as i made myself available to be used
by forces i desperately sought to understand. i heard hope

whispering through the needles of the southern pine trees during the late fifties and i gave it voice. that does not mean i always knew what i was saying. that does not mean i understood the depth and extent of the transformations with which everyone now wants to credit me.

hi-story is the imperceptible accretion of private acts and silent gestures, of separate and solitary decisions to do something today that you would not have yesterday. our sense of humanity and its possibilities expands and contracts as we decide each day how much beauty we will permit to pour through our voices.

❖

"Blacks did not hate whites then. We were black and white together, as we sang in 'We Shall Overcome.' White southerners were right. The civil rights movement *was* about mixing the races. How could it have been otherwise? If keeping the races separate was the problem, mixing them had to be the solution.

"But something happened and blacks became racist. I'm not supposed to say that, am I? But I can't rationalize and call the current black antipathy to whites 'antiracism racism,' or some such doublespeak. Being black does not confer automatic immunity from being racist.

"I miss the innocence of black and white together. Innocence is as much a knowledge as experience. We deride innocence as unworthy of maturity, but we need it to safeguard us. Without innocence, experience makes us cynics.

"Until the four children were murdered in the bombing of the church in Birmingham in 1963, nobody told me I couldn't know what it was like to be black. People were eager for me to know, eager for me to come into their homes and listen to their stories. The black experience was not an exclusive preserve like beachfront property. No one thought there was anything to gain by putting a NO TRESPASSING sign on his race."

But blacks no longer cared that there had also been whites in the civil rights movement who had inhaled and exhaled mortality with the monotonous regularity of their heartbeats and, three decades later, had been left alone with the pain of neglected idealism and the shame of murdered hope.

Elizabeth did not want a parade or a plaque, but she resented the contempt and derision of a generation of blacks still in diapers when Cal was killed, a generation of *African-Americans* who had become mesmerized by the melodious knell of victimhood.

"What happened? How did we get from 'We Shall Overcome' to 'It's a Black Thing'?" Elizabeth whispered earnestly.

In those lonely last months of his life, Cal understood as little as she did now. He had become an anachronism before his very eyes, he who had single-handedly demonstrated against bus segregation in Atlanta, boarding buses and sitting alone in the white sections and being beaten by whites, arrested, beaten a second time by policemen, and the first opportunity after getting out of jail or the hospital, he was back on the buses. Rifle shots were fired into his home one night barely missing Andrea. On another, a bomb exploded at the front half of his house seconds after Andrea had walked into the back. Yet he had stood amid the smoking rubble and calmed a crowd of angry blacks aching for the catharsis of retaliatory violence. He was 31 years old, a philosophy professor at Spelman, but he articulated the black cry for freedom with the accent of the Alabama minister's son he was and the sophistication of the philosopher-savior he was becoming. He took the suffering of years when hope lay stillborn in watery ditches and melded it with the dignity of fortitude that would not be shattered during nights when stars fell and days when the sun stood still. There had never been a figure quite like him, a black man who could quote Plato in Greek and, in the next breath, sing a country blues, who was as comfortable eating pâté with President Kennedy in the White House as he was eating ham and grits with redeye gravy in a sharecropper's cabin.

"Bobby had saved a seat for me in the balcony in the middle of the first row," she resumed aloud, unaware that she had been vocally silent. "I looked down to the high-backed chairs on the pulpit and there, in the middle, directly in front of me sat John Calvin Marshall.

"He was leaning to his right, listening to the college president speaking quietly in his ear. However, his eyes looked out into the chapel at the students coming in with little of their usual noise and talking."

She paused. "This is where it gets hard, Andrea. I want you to understand, but not because I want your forgiveness. I committed no sin and therefore do not need absolution. People want adultery to be a morality play in which virtue always resides with the wife. But an adulterous *love* is moral. I don't know that a loveless monogamy is."

She stopped, sighed, inhaled deeply, held the breath for a moment, then let it out slowly.

"I have never spoken of my relationship with Cal. For the seven years we were together and the twenty-five since he was assassinated, I have kept hidden that which gave my life meaning.

"I never wanted to share it, even if that had been possible. Who would have understood? I continue to love him and care for him. Death is a momentary interruption of a relationship. Nothing more."

Her vision was blurred by the shock of unanticipated tears. She heard herself sniff and waited until she was sure she could speak without a tremor in her voice.

"He looks up at me. A blond white girl in a chapel of a thousand black students stands out. A picture of me being arrested had appeared on the front page of the *New York Times* and every other paper in America.

"I did not know he was looking for me as he watched the students come in. But when his eyes found me, I knew. At least my body did.

"My father used to think I had ESP. I do not. I just pay attention to the flashes of light rather than wait for the beams.

"I was ten and was in the backseat of the car, looking out the window. The sky was getting dark. Without thinking, I told my parents we should buy some candles because the electricity was going to go out. My father, the most rational and logical of men who used that steel trap of a mind to make more money than I'll spend in this lifetime, believed me. Mother did not. He stopped and bought candles and kerosene lamps. Mother said he was spoiling me, indulging me. The storm came and the electricity went out; my mother never trusted me again.

"I was seventeen and was driving along a street. I had not had my license long. Suddenly I had a feeling I should get out of the car. I pulled over and ran. A moment later, the car burst into flames. How many times after a plane crash do you read about someone who was supposed to be on the plane but he or she 'had a feeling' and decided to take another flight?

"I try to grasp the tiny feelings that dart past like insects on the surface of a still pond. So it was when he looked at me that morning.

"It was not love at first sight. If it had been, less would

have been required of me. But love is not as much a feeling as it is a decision about who or what you admit into your soul. When he looked at me, I was not deceived by the composed exterior of John Calvin Marshall. I, that is, my body, experienced his loneliness and terror at being John Calvin Marshall, and it, I admitted him, and the loneliness, and the terror into my soul.

"That was the defining moment of my life. I knew it then. Our eyes met, and I wanted to look away, but I chose to hold his eyes with mine.

"Then, the college president stood to introduce him and Cal looked away. A moment later, as the college president called his name and he rose from the high-backed chair, the student body leaped to its feet and applauded. I looked around the chapel into the faces of the black students gleaming with anticipated salvation. These were my classmates, girls on my floor in Jubilee Hall, boys I sat beside in class, and I realized that I did not know them. The hope and longing and pain in their applause frightened me. The blue of my eyes, the yellow of my hair, the roseate paleness of my skin insulated me from danger and placed me outside the suffering and therefore outside the need for deliverance. Yet, being outside did not mean I was alienated. Because I did not share the particularity of that moment did not mean I could not care.

"Cal stood at the podium, his hands grasping its sides. He was dressed in a dark suit cut narrowly to emphasize his slim frame. He was the medium-brown color of oak leaves in November, and looked just as ordinary, neither especially handsome or repugnant, without mustache or goatee. Nothing about him indicated he was the man inspiring a generation of black, and soon, white youth to live as if ideals were as tangible as money and infinitely more important.

"Expressionless, his body still, he seemed annoyed by the

applause and his eyes flitted around the chapel like a bird in a room unable to distinguish solid wall from open window. But when his eyes darted quickly up to the balcony, mine were waiting and for an instant, long enough for me to notice, he rested.

"When the applause stopped and we sat down, he began to speak. His voice was soft and deep, the tone almost lazy as if he had learned that a spoken lullaby could be more musical than one sung. In the years to come, I would hear countless speeches begin with the painfully slow cadences that caused some to wonder if he was on medication. 'Ladies and gentle-men. ———— It is ———— with ———— great ———— plea——sure ———— that I come to tell you ———— the Negro ———— will no longer be ———— a slave ———— to any white man.' He said it calmly, matter-of-factly, lazily, and the very disinterestedness of the tone made the applause and stomping of feet and cheering even more raucous and prolonged. Others thought the lethargy of his beginning was a way of measuring the temperature of the audience, but I recognized those long silences as spaces in which the man I would come to love as Cal receded and John Calvin Marshall came to the fore. As his cadence became more regular, an ordinary man became the apotheosis of four centuries of history written in red tears and salty blood. Imperceptibly, the cadence quickened and the timbre of his voice echoed back to stubbled fields where Nat Turner and Denmark Vesey sang fired songs of burning freedom, back to the *lap-slap* of ocean against the hulls of white-masted slave ships cleaving the waves with cargos of soul and flesh, back to muffled sobs and deafening screams, the rhythms of broken hearts beating in whole bodies.

" 'Our struggle,' he shouted at the end, his voice rising with the majesty and power of a wave, 'is for the redemption of the unquiet soul of the slave *and* the unquiet soul of the slaveowner because black man and white man are the front and back of the same soul, two halves, which together make a harmonious whole but apart can only create dissonance, discord and dissension. Walk together, children. Don't you get weary. There's a great camp meeting in the promised land.'

"Applause rained down on him like rice on a bride. As if being awakened, his eyes blinked and the terror and loneliness returned, only this time with a desperation that had not been there before. He looked as if he did not know who was being applauded, or why. Then he raised his head, his eyes deliberately seeking mine this time. Instinctively I knew he would need me, and when our eyes met, I saw his relief and saw his body relax as he returned to himself. He looked away as the college president came up to shake his hand. But I held him in my eyes for a moment longer.

"Having sat at the front row of the balcony, Bobby and I were practically the last to leave. As we came down the steps into the foyer, Cal was entering it from the chapel. He was surrounded by students but he saw me and stopped.

"Students turned to see what had drawn his attention. 'It's Lisa,' voices whispered.

" 'Stand back and let Lisa through,' someone said. I wanted to run back up the stairs because I was afraid that if anyone saw us together they would think we were lovers. Such had been the extent of the intimacy we had exchanged without word or touch."

Elizabeth played idly with the diamond ring on the third finger of her left hand. When Gregory had proposed and offered it to her, she had been disappointed. Not by the ring. It was gorgeous. Her disappointment was that Gregory had needed to buy one so clearly beyond his means as a young dentist. He wanted to impress her, she who could afford whatever she wanted. She let him put the ring on her finger but made a silent decision to keep their finances separate. However, she had been embarrassed that wearing the ring had made her feel special and apart from all the women who did not wear this sign of chosenness.

Such a silly little emotion, the need to feel special and apart. She wondered that the black girls at Fisk had not hated her.

"*We* don't have a choice about sitting-in," Bobby explained one evening later that spring as they walked across campus. "You do and you chose to go to jail, risk getting beat up, cursed, spit at. That's why we love you. That's why you're special to us."

She had been the white girl who crossed the color line. Her picture on the front page of the *New York Times* had given the protests legitimacy in the eyes of other whites. "Among those arrested was Lisa Adams, 20-year-old daughter of wealthy businessman and inventor, Phelps Adams."

"When the picture appeared in the paper," she said aloud, "Jessica, my mother, called and wanted to know what did I think I was doing? Back then I got rattled pretty quickly when asked to explain myself and the more I tried the harder it was to think. This made me appear even more stupid, which frustrated and infuriated Jessica, and within two minutes I was crying hysterically. Swimming Niagara Falls and surviving would have been infinitely easier for Jessica than navigating through tears, especially those of her only child. To Jessica my tears were a negative commentary on her parenting. She was right about that. Never have tears been filled with as much anger and hatred as those I shed in her presence. She gave the phone to Daddy. For him, my tears were merely language in search of an alphabet.

"He got on the phone and didn't ask me how I was or what I was crying about. Instead, he asked, casually, 'How was the train ride?' "

"I wanted to yell at him, 'What do you mean, how was the train ride? Don't you see I'm upset? Didn't you see my picture in the paper? Are you proud of me or are you angry, too? And, anyway, I told you right after I got here that the train ride was fine. What do you want?'

"But I trusted Daddy not to ask an inconsequential question. So, I started talking about the cactus in Arizona and we reminisced about the Polo Club in Phoenix where I first started to learn golf and soon I wasn't crying because I was back on the train coming to Nashville.

"As I relived the ride I remembered looking out the window as the train brought me closer and closer to Nashville. I had no idea why I was on that train. The last place I belonged was on an exchange program to a small Negro college in the South. Only the social-conscious, political, liberal kids chose one of the Negro schools in the South. I had a reputation on campus as a beach bunny and a ski bunny, which was unfair. I was an athlete but, in those days, such status was too high to accord a woman. But my professors knew: when it was snowing in the mountains or the surf was up, expecting me in class was like telling a hawk not to soar. So, people were incredulous when they heard that not only was I going on exchange but I was going to a Negro school in the South.

"It was Daddy's suggestion. With a name like Phelps Adams, it's safe to assume he had roots in New England, Vermont to be exact. Some great grandmother or great aunt had been one of the New England school marms who went South after the Civil War to teach the freed slaves and had ended up at what was then called Fisk Normal School. When

Daddy saw Fisk's name on the list of exchange schools, he wanted me to go. So, I did.

"I told Daddy about getting off the train in Nashville after the three-day ride and seeing a sign that said WHITE ENTRANCE and another that said COLORED ENTRANCE. I had no idea what was going on. Then I had trouble getting a cab because the white cab drivers wouldn't take me to Fisk, and there were no Negro cabs around. Finally, someone from Fisk arrived.

"During my first week I saw signs whenever I went downtown. COLORED RESTROOM. COLORED WATER. NO COLORED ALLOWED. WHITE ONLY. I asked my roommate to go downtown on the bus with me and she refused and I couldn't understand why until she said we couldn't sit together because we would be arrested. Why? I asked. That's just how it is, I was told.

"As I told all this to Daddy, it became clear why I went on the sit-ins and got arrested. I didn't like the law telling me where I had to sit on a bus and that I couldn't eat in a restaurant with whomever I wanted to. There was nothing political about it. Segregation put limits on my life. Gregory says I take things too personally. But how else can I take them? I exist in the world as a person."

History is subjective experience, she had told him when they met that summer of 1969, that summer she spent wondering how she could live and why she should, now that Cal was dead.

She remembered driving alone from Atlanta to Nashville after they took his body from her arms, remembered making a statement to the police, and then, what? She was supposed to just get in the truck and go? But how? It would have helped if there had been someone to say "I'm sorry," someone to ask, "Is there anything I can do for you?" But those words were reserved for Andrea, the titular wife. So, she eventually turned the key in the truck's ignition, Cal's blood still damp on her blouse, and drove out of the hotel parking lot.

When she reached her house in Nashville, she went to bed and slept for most of three days, getting up only to go to the bathroom and drink water or orange juice and watch the news on TV. She remembered seeing Cal's funeral and the procession of mourners walking from the church to the cemetery behind Cal's plain wooden coffin carried on the shoulders of six black men. Andrea was in the center of the picture, her face covered by a veil. Lisa wondered if Cal's spirit wondered where she was, needed her to be there even now.

But she was white and there was no place for her anymore in the civil rights movement, what little of it remained in the tide of blackness washing ashore as if the souls of the African dead thrown overboard from slave ships now sought succor. She would not stay and become the object of a scorn she had not earned. But where to go and what to do? After TV coverage of the funeral ended, she went back to bed and was still trapped in sleep the next morning when a loud knocking awakened her.

She opened the door and there he was, tall and proper, the hair more gray than black now. What did he think of his daughter and her picture on the front of every newspaper and magazine in the world holding the dying body of John Calvin Marshall? Had he been suspicious? He never said. He never asked. He opened his arms and she fell against him and he folded her into himself and she cried for the first time.

Later, that morning, after he shopped and came back and cooked for her, he asked if she wanted to come home. She cried again because home was Cal and Cal was now memory of heartbeat.

She had looked around at her little house hidden in a grove of trees on a backroad north of Nashville. It had taken her a while to find a place secluded enough so Cal could come without being seen. A search of the records had uncovered an owner in Florida who was all too happy to sell the abandoned shack and the ten acres surrounding it. She had the house rebuilt, a little bigger but not much. She had not wanted her existence there to become the object of curious attention.

She came to love its simplicity — the living room one walked into from the outside, the kitchen/dining area directly behind, and to the left off the kitchen, the bedroom and bath. No one had ever come there except Cal.

That afternoon she looked at her house and noticed for the first time that it was devoid of objects that would have made vivid whom she had been for the past seven years. There were no stuffed animals, no posters evoking memories of vacations taken or fantasized, no paintings crystallizing an essence of soul aching to be lived, no shelves of records and books to mark the solitary pleasures where senses met mind and neither resented the other.

It was empty because only emptiness offered a respite from the companionship of death more constant than any love.

MAY 7, 1955: BELZONI, MISSISSIPPI — REVEREND GEORGE LEE. 52. MURDERED FOR ORGANIZING NEGROES TO VOTE. SHERIFF CONCLUDES LEE DIED IN A TRAFFIC ACCIDENT. WHEN PRESENTED WITH THE LEAD SHOTGUN PELLETS TAKEN FROM LEE'S FACE, SHERIFF SAYS THEY LOOK LIKE DENTAL FILLINGS.

AUGUST 13, 1955: BROOKHAVEN, MISSISSIPPI — LAMAR SMITH, 63, MURDERED. "I'M SURE IF THERE WAS ANY REASON FOR THE

AND ALL OUR WOUNDS FORGIVEN

SHOOTING IT WAS THAT SMITH THOUGHT HE WAS AS GOOD AS ANY WHITE MAN," SAID A WHITE FRIEND OF SMITH'S.

AUGUST 28, 1955: MONEY, MISSISSIPPI — EMMETT TILL, 14, MURDERED FOR SPEAKING TO A WHITE WOMAN.

JANUARY 23, 1957: MONTGOMERY, ALABAMA — WILLIE EDWARDS, JR., 25, FORCED AT GUNPOINT TO JUMP FROM A BRIDGE INTO THE ALABAMA RIVER. IN 1966, ALABAMA ATTORNEY GENERAL ARRESTS THREE MEN FOR THE MURDER. JUDGE FRANK EMBRY RULES THAT "FORCING A PERSON TO JUMP FROM A BRIDGE DOES NOT NATURALLY AND PROBABLY LEAD TO THE DEATH OF SUCH PERSON." CASE HAS TO BE DROPPED.

The dead were referred to so often in conversation there was no clear demarcation between the realm of the living and those who inhabited one beyond. Negroes in the South permitted their dead to walk among them — as long as they behaved themselves — and those dead whose dying had been a crucifixion, those dead whose dying had no other source than the color of their skin, those dead for whom the grieving never stopped, those were the ones whose names it was important to weave into daily speech, because speaking their names and recounting their dying was a way of caring for and loving them, a way of easing the pain of the living and the dead.

APRIL 25, 1959: POPLARVILLE, MISSISSIPPI — MACK CHARLES PARKER, 23, TAKEN FROM JAIL AND LYNCHED. A VETERAN, PARKER WAS ARRESTED FOR RAPE THOUGH THE VICTIM WAS UNSURE HE WAS HER ATTACKER. WHITES WERE ANGERED THAT PARKER'S COFFIN WAS DRAPED WITH AN AMERICAN FLAG. VETERANS ADMINISTRATION ORDERS PARKER'S SISTER TO RETURN IT.

SEPTEMBER 25, 1961: HERBERT LEE, 50, SHOT AND KILLED BY E.H. HURST, A MISSISSIPPI REPRESENTATIVE. LEE HAD BEEN WORKING TO REGISTER BLACKS TO VOTE.

APRIL 9, 1962: TAYLORSVILLE, MISSISSIPPI — CPL. ROMAN DUCKS- WORTH, JR., 28, A MILITARY POLICEMAN, RECEIVES EMERGENCY LEAVE FROM THE ARMY TO BE HOME WITH HIS WIFE AFTER THE DELIVERY OF THEIR SIXTH CHILD. DUCKSWORTH IS ASLEEP WHEN BUS PULLS INTO HIS HOMETOWN OF TAYLORSVILLE. POLICE OFFICER WILLIAM KELLY THINKS DUCKSWORTH MIGHT BE A 'FREEDOM RIDER' AND SHOOTS HIM. LATER, OFFICER KELLY SENDS MESSAGE TO CPL. DUCKSWORTH'S FATHER, SAYING, IF HE HAD KNOWN WHOSE SON IT WAS, "I WOULDN'T HAVE SHOT HIM." DUCKSWORTH'S FATHER SENDS MESSAGE BACK: "I DON'T CARE WHOSE SON IT WAS, YOU HAD NO BUSINESS SHOOTING HIM."

SEPTEMBER 30, 1962: OXFORD, MISSISSIPPI — PAUL GUIHARD, 30, FRENCH REPORTER, SHOT IN THE BACK AND KILLED WHILE COVERING THE RIOTS AT OLE MISS WHEN JAMES MEREDITH ADMITTED AS FIRST BLACK STUDENT.

APRIL 23, 1963: ATTALLA, ALABAMA — WILLIAM MOORE, 36, A WHITE SUBSTITUTE MAIL CARRIER FROM BALTIMORE, IS MURDERED AS HE WALKS FROM CHATTANOOGA, TENNESSEE, TO JACKSON, MISSISSIPPI, CARRYING A SANDWICH BOARD READING "EAT AT JOE'S — BLACK AND WHITE".

JUNE 12, 1963: JACKSON, MISSISSIPPI — MEDGAR EVERS, 38, MISSISSIPPI NAACP LEADER, SHOT AND KILLED IN HIS DRIVEWAY.

❖

i was not shocked or outraged by the evil. i was never a sentimentalist about the capacity of the human animal to inflict pain and death and justify it. those who are dismayed by atrocities indulge their emotions and reveal their ignorance of history or refusal to regard it seriously. much of man's energy is expended on ways to luxuriate in the sensuality of death.

there is a town in mississippi called drew. i believe it is the hometown of some pro quarterback from the seventies or eighties. a negro woman in drew told me that when she was a girl there was a lynching in the town. the negro was castrated. his penis was put in a large jar of alcohol and kept in the window of the general store for many years afterward. such stories were not rare in the south.

i was not surprised, dismayed, outraged, indignant or angered by american atrocities and massacres in vietnam, or anyone else's atrocities for that matter. neither did i ever sign any of the self-serving full page ads decrying this or that injustice that appeared with the regularity of bowel movements in the pages of the new york times. the intellectuals, artists and academics who were signatories actually thought they were discharging a moral debt by affixing their names to those self-righteous proclamations. assuaging one's conscience is not a moral act. it is an evasion of responsibility for the wounds each of us inflicts. it is an evasion of responsibility for the wounds we suffer.

i did not want to denounce evil. i wanted to understand. i wanted to understand how a person decides to bomb a church on a sunday morning. does it come to you while having a donut and coffee? are you sitting on your front porch one saturday afternoon sipping iced tea and think, shit, i believe i'll go bomb a nigger church sunday. probably be a lot of little kids in there and maybe three or four of them will get killed. did the person or persons who made that decision sleep as well as harry truman?

i wanted to understand how truman could have slept so soundly. why didn't he lie awake for a few moments? why wasn't there at least one stitch of remorse?

harry truman is the quintessential twentieth-century man. the buck stops here, read the little sign on his desk. all words. all words. it is not enough to accept responsibility for making a decision. we must also accept responsibility for the consequences of that decision, even the consequences we did not anticipate and could not have foreseen. otherwise the buck does not stop. it simply passes to the next generation. all acts have consequences.

example:
during the late fifties and early sixties, fast food restaurants — mcdonald's, kentucky fried chicken, pizza hut — began opening across the country. at one time eating out had been a special event, a luxury permitted only on mother's day or easter. with the proliferation of fast food franchises, eating out became a way of life. in its tv ads mcdonald's portrayed itself as a substitute for home. the smiles of the girls behind the counter were an instant infusion of mother love, love real moms could no longer give after a hard day at the office. the mothers were now in need of mothers and an institution that offered hot food at a reasonable price between five and seven p.m. was a good enough substitute.

so convenience joined saving time as a primary value in american life. the ease of accomplishing an end became an unquestioned good. (i suppose one could say dropping the

bomb on hiroshima was convenient. though not for the japanese.) i was not opposed to convenience. but convenience
costs.

when i was a child i would go to the chicken yard behind
our house, catch a hen and with a hatchet, take off its head.
once the chicken was dead, i carried its warm and bloody
carcass into the kitchen where my mother dropped it into a
large pot of boiling water and took off the feathers. i don't
remember when it became "more convenient" to buy
chicken at the store, already defeathered and cut up,
wrapped tightly in cellophane. of course, for city people there
was no alternative. but being able to buy a chicken in the
grocery store removed us one step from relationship with
the living creature that provided us food. but because we
cooked it we still handled the breasts and thighs and legs.
when we ate the chicken we saw the blood next to the bone
if the chicken had been undercooked, and both my mother
and andrea consistently did that. now it is "more convenient"
to go to a fast food franchise where every piece of chicken
is fried to the same degree of doneness each and every
time. a child grows up without any sense that once, those
plump thighs and legs walked and ran.

perhaps this did not matter. i assumed something was
gained by active participation in the process of feeding oneself. i assumed something was lost by becoming someone
who merely consumed.

even if my assumptions were mistaken, convenience is not
a value that should be at the heart of a nation's culture. a
child who grows up being taught that convenience is the
greater good will seek convenience in areas where it cannot
obtain. love is not a convenience. parenting is constant in-

convenience. ethics are inconvenient. and believe me, death is most inconvenient of all.

did i want to turn back the clock and have us hunt and kill our own food? not at all. i merely wanted us to be as aware as humanly possible of what we did. accepting responsibility for the consequences we could not have foreseen was to acknowledge our limitations. it was to suffer our finiteness. it was to know that we and the chicken shared an identical condition — mortality. i wanted us to suffer our mortality.

if i do not suffer the infuriating pain of and rage at my own mortality, then I will seek to make you die in my stead. like the natives of preliterate cultures who believed they acquired something of the spirit of the bear or deer when they killed it, i have wondered if our wars are not a spiritual cannibalism. americans feast on death because they fear life. and they hate their fear.

❖

SEPTEMBER 15, 1963: BIRMINGHAM, ALABAMA
ADDIE MAE COLLINS, 14
DENISE MCNAIR, 11
CYNTHIA WESLEY, 14
CAROLE ROBERTSON, 14
MURDERED IN BOMBING OF SIXTEENTH STREET BAPTIST CHURCH.

SAME DAY, SAME CITY: VIRGIL WARE, 13, IS RIDING ON THE HANDLEBARS OF HIS BROTHER'S BICYCLE WHEN HE IS SHOT AND KILLED BY TWO WHITE TEENAGERS IN A TRUCK. TWO 16-YEAR OLD EAGLE SCOUTS ARE ARRESTED AND CHARGED WITH MANSLAUGHTER.

THEY ARE CONVICTED. ONE SERVES SEVEN MONTHS. THE OTHER IS
RELEASED AFTER A FEW DAYS AND WARNED BY THE JUDGE NOT TO
HAVE ANOTHER "LAPSE."

JANUARY 31, 1964: LIBERTY, MISSISSIPPI — LOUIS ALLEN, 45, BLACK
WITNESS TO MURDER OF HERBERT LEE, SHOT AND KILLED.

People talked of death more often than of love, talked of
it matter-of-factly. Finding bodies of black men in rivers was
a part of the natural order of things in the South, but she
never learned to laugh and joke about it, never learned, like
Cal, to walk easy with Death by her side, or like others, to
drive at maniacal speeds over midnight highways mocking
Death as if it were a bull with razor sharp horns and she the
toreador and cape and the object was not to kill the bull —
that was not possible — but to see how long she could remain
alive.

The bareness of her house had provided a hiding place
from Death as omnipresent in her landscape as a fat and
silly full moon on the face of a perpetual night. When she
was there, she was able to forget and felt guilty because Cal
could never forget and neither could any of the other blacks
in the civil rights movement and she had asked Cal if it was
all right if she forgot sometimes. It was unavoidable. When
she walked along a street in downtown Nashville, her height
or her looks may have called attention to her but not her
color.

"I need you to be white and blond and blue-eyed," he
had said.

She left the house. A few years later someone found her
name in the records and she sold the house and land for a
large profit to a development corporation that was going to
put up — what else? — a mall.

She returned with her father to the house in California

where she had grown up and where her parents now lived in dignified estrangement. When she went into what had been her room, she was surprised to find it almost as bare as the house in Nashville. She had not put pictures of movie stars on her walls or collected stuffed animals, or read books besides the ones needed for school. The only furniture was a king-sized bed and a dresser. The room, and it was a large one, was dominated by the sliding glass doors leading to a deck from which stairs led down to the beach. The wall at a right angle to the doors was a floor-to-ceiling mirror. The floors were polished, gleaming with the hard, flinty brightness of the sun off the ocean. Had she never had enough life to depict with objects, or had she always needed respite from the omnipresence of death?

"So. You're back."

She turned at the flat sound of Jessica's voice. The two women looked at each other with the kind of matter-of-fact hatred only possible between mother and daughter, a hatred that came not from things done by each to the other but that flowed from who they were, a hatred so natural that neither had to expend emotion on it, a hatred so intimate that it was a kind of love.

"Jessica," Elizabeth said. She could not remember the last time she had seen or talked on the phone with her mother but it had been too long. The woman standing in the doorway looked twenty years older than her fifty-two years. The body was still tall and erect (and she had never noticed how much alike her father and Jessica looked) and the skin of the lean face was still taut, but there was a weariness of spirit in the eyes, a nimbus of bankruptcy in the straight set of the lips that would have given her the appearance of evil had there been any vitality left. Elizabeth wondered if she was going to die soon. (She did.)

"How long are you staying?"

"Why?"

"I don't know. Just making conversation, I guess. What would you like me to ask you? What it was like being the mistress of one of the most famous men of the twentieth century? Is it true what they say about black men's penises? What would you like me to say?"

Elizabeth was too spent and, surprisingly, too mature to grab the bait as she would have in years past. "Would you care to join me for a walk on the beach, Jessica?" she asked instead.

The older woman hesitated, then nodded.

That summer of 1969 was lived more outdoors than in. She walked the beach for hours, sometimes with Jessica, sometimes with her father, most of the time alone, especially at dusk when she would cry and scream into the roar of the surf. She was surprised at how insignificant the world became in the midst of grief. She was aware of the riots across the country after Cal's death, and there was an evening when she sat with her father and Jessica and watched Neil Armstrong take a small step for man and a giant one for mankind and she thought how presumptuous of him to think he knew the significance of being the first person on the moon. There was something that summer about a young woman drowning in a car driven by Ted Kennedy but she didn't think about the political implications for the presidential ambitions of the last Kennedy brother. Her grief merged with that of the young woman's parents and she wept for both. She cried, too, when she saw a magazine photo from a large rock festival at some place back east called Woodstock and in one a beautiful young woman with long blond hair sat on the shoulders of a guy and both were bare chested and it was raining and they were so happy and Elizabeth was sorry that she had never been so young and so free, that she had never been in love and felt the rain on her breasts as she rode astride her lover's shoulders.

All summer she weaved back and forth across the yellow line separating grief and self-pity, sometimes aware vaguely that grief did not make her unique in human history, or worthy of notice or comment. But the pain of grief also encompasses all of history, and, in her self-pity, she belonged to humanity more completely than she ever had.

She permitted her father to coax her out for drives down the coast to La Jolla or up to Santa Barbara and through reading bumper stickers she became aware of a nation pirouetting into self-pity, an emotion tolerable in a person — for a while — but for a nation, the aggrieved self-righteousness at the core of self-pity was potentially volatile and dangerous.

OUR GOD ISN'T DEAD, SORRY ABOUT YOURS

TRUST GOD! SHE PROVIDES

WE ARE THE SILENT MAJORITY

HELP YOUR POLICE FIGHT CRIME

WE ARE THE PEOPLE OUR PARENTS WARNED US ABOUT

TARZAN AND JANE ARE LIVING IN SIN

CUSTER WORE AN ARROW SHIRT

The evening she met Gregory she supposed she had been well across the yellow line and breaking the speed limit in the self-pity lane.

She had been sitting just above the tide line, staring across the dark evening blue of the ocean when suddenly, a voice, "Pardon me. Are you Lisa Adams?"

She looked up into a face as young as love.

"Who are you?" she asked, her voice sounding sharp and unfriendly in her ears.

"I'm sorry. Greg. Gregory Townley. I'm spending the summer at the Carver's," he pointed down the beach and up the cliff.

She shook her head. "I don't know the neighbors."

"I'll be entering my first year of dentistry school at UCLA. Reg Carver and I were roommates at USC and will be also at dental school, and he invited me to stay the summer with him and his folks rather than going halfway across the country to Chicago, my home, where I wouldn't know anybody anymore. Do you mind if I sit down?"

She wanted to say no, but he seemed harmless enough.

"I saw your picture in the paper when —" he hesitated, not knowing how to finish the sentence.

"John Calvin Marshall was killed," she finished it for him. She looked at him, his developed chest, the legs that seemed muscled and resilient, and wondered if he were strong enough to ride her on his shoulders, her thighs clasping his cheeks, her breasts open to the sun, the wind and the rain.

And that was how it began, like most relationships, in a fantasy of being through an other someone she had never been. Gregory looked — and how voluptuous the word sounded — normal. It appeared to her that Death did not even know his name yet, that Death was not aware that this Gregory existed and maybe, just maybe, he might live forever, gazing at her shyly, starstruck because she, she — and what was his fantasy of whom he would become through her?

"What was John Calvin Marshall like?" he asked without prelude. "I'm sorry. You don't have to answer if that's too personal."

"And what made you think I did have to answer?"

"I didn't mean it quite the way it sounded," he apologized. "And it is certainly none of my business. But I'll probably never again in my life be this close to someone who knew him."

"Why do you want to know?"

He shrugged. "I guess you wonder what's real about these people on TV and what isn't. And the only one who knows is someone who sees them off-camera, as it were."

"Maybe the one you see on television is the real one, and the person off-camera is unreal," she responded, not caring to answer his question.

"What is your definition of real?"

"Whatever people agree to."

He thought for a moment. "Are you saying reality is subjective?"

She thought for a moment. "Yes, I think I am."

"An aching tooth is not subjective."

"An *abscessed* tooth is not subjective. The aching is."

He smiled. "Touché!"

"I won't answer your question except to say that John Calvin Marshall was someone I cared about — deeply, but I felt no anger when he was killed. It was an inevitability he lived with. For most blacks, however, John Calvin Marshall was the best in them. Killing him killed something in all black America. Why else were there riots all across the country? Blacks were expressing the grief of their own deaths."

"I disagree," Gregory interrupted. "There are a lot of whites like me who are in shock and think Marshall's death is the worst thing that could have happened."

She nodded. "Sure, a lot of white people are deeply grieved, but they don't feel as if that which gave their lives definition and meaning and direction has been taken away. And that's the problem. The civil rights movement was successful because at the same moment in time and in the same places, the subjective experiences of blacks and whites concurred with the notion that an integrated society was in everyone's best interest. Now, the subjective experiences of blacks and whites have diverged. For blacks the best among them has been killed by the worst among whites. Without John Calvin Marshall I wonder if all of us, black and white, will lose faith that we can ever be better than we are."

"I do take things personally," she resumed, aloud to Andrea. "How else can something have substance? How else can I have a relationship to it? If there is no relationship, there is no reality, no existence."

Cal lived in terror that one day when the audiences and TV cameras and radio microphones and reporters with their pads were gone, he — Cal — would not awaken because John Calvin Marshall would have swallowed him and killed all memory of person and solitude. He clung to her body and remembered himself.

That Thursday morning in the foyer of the chapel, she stood at the bottom of the stairs and waited for him to come to her. It was a self-assurance of tissue and bone, marrow and muscle and blood.

At five-ten, she was a physical presence, exuding mastery of the spot on which she stood. She lived in her body as if it were an instrument that registered the hidden tremors of souls and bestowed the intimacy of grace.

"Cal was tall enough to look me directly in the eyes, and his eyes did not leave mine to seek out my body. He didn't

smile and I was pleased he knew I didn't need him to put me at ease. He did not proffer his hand.
" 'So, you're Elizabeth,' he said.

"No one, not even my parents, called me Elizabeth. That same afternoon I went to the library and looked up the *New York Times* with my picture in it. They had called me Lisa. "*He* called me Elizabeth.

"I dissect moments as if they are specimens in a zoology class. Maybe Gregory and I aren't so different after all. He x-rays decisions; I cut into a single moment of conversation and peel back the layers of silence, the sinews of intonation, the spongy tissues of words until I see the throbbing muscle of the heart.

"That's what lovers do. They return to moments in their histories and search out the nuances of feeling of which they had been unaware. They share the thoughts not expressed for the sake of those that more needed saying. By ferreting out the latent, their love is animated in ever new ways.

"How many times over the years I have returned to that moment in the foyer of the chapel searching for shadows of emotion. One specter I have uncovered is an embarrassment that he focussed his attention on me and excluded you. I saw you at the edge of the semicircle of students around him. You looked more like a graduate student than Mrs. John Calvin Marshall.

"Looking at you, I knew you and he were not married. No man married in his soul would risk trusting that soul with another woman, and that was what Cal was doing, with you looking on. If he had been interested only in my body, that would have been another matter. Men are not discriminate about whom they share their bodies with. I suppose I would be the same if my sex organ hung from my torso like a nightmare, if I had to touch it several times a day, if it went from limpness to hardness of its own volition, imposing its presence on my consciousness when I was not expecting it and did not want it. Having a penis must be like living with an alien being, a parasite that attaches itself to you and leads you around seeking its own gratification. So what if you've got a wife and four kids at home and you love them dearly? What's love when there's pussy to be had?"

"I knew he was not with you because I had been with Jessica and father in social settings often, had seen her dressed in nonexistence with a smile as women surrounded my father. Most men are not married to their wives, not if marriage is one soul living in two bodies. Most women live in anger, alone in their souls, alone in their bodies."

Elizabeth gazed on Andrea and envied the iconic dignity in her face. Age would not usher Elizabeth into such a hallowed visage. She was merely beautiful and beauty was a caprice of Nature — an eighth of an inch added to or missing from a lip, an infinitesimal curl to the ends of the lashes, a lift to the curve of the cheekbone as insubstantial as a dusting of snow on ice. The difference between beauty and ugliness was thinner than a fingernail.

At 51 Elizabeth still carried herself with the ease of one comfortable in her skin. The hair was shorter now and streaked with gray strands, which she regarded as laurel wreaths earned in the freedom of truth. She had become what was called a "striking-looking" woman, meaning people saw her and wondered if she was "somebody." Her height, the blond hair, the almond-shaped blue eyes, the almost perfectly shaped nose and lips, and, on that day in the hospital, the wide, soft suede skirt with two deep pockets, the matching boots of a leather soft enough that the tops could be folded and were, the white cable-stitch sweater turned over at the neck gave her the look of a well-to-do, very competent, yet down-to-earth woman who moved through the world with an assurance most women believed they could never attain and men longed to have for themselves.

She feared that with age the flesh would expand and sag, and cheekbone and turn-of-lip and curve-of-lash would fade into folds of skin, while wrinkles, like tread marks, would reveal the weight of the vehicles that had passed in the nights.

"You look as if no vehicles passed through your nights, Andrea. You look as if you never cried in the darkness. That cannot be. What was it like when they called and told you Cal had been assassinated? Were you relieved the waiting was finally over? Or were you surprised it had actually happened, surprised someone had dared kill John Calvin Marshall? And what was it like when you turned on the television and saw the film of his dying body being held lovingly against my breasts, saw me holding him with that subtle familiarity of touch that comes only after a thousand nights of touches? I was explained away as his 'longtime personal secretary.' But it is one thing to know your husband is sleeping with another woman. It is quite another to see him lying in her arms, dying."

She wished her fingers were like the silicon chips of computers that remembered whatever was put onto them and, with a keystroke, or the click of a computer mouse, memory was restored. There, somewhere, in the whorls of her fingertips was the softness of his flesh, the tight curls of his hair, the fullness of his lips. What command would access what was now dust?

Elizabeth looked back at the woman in the bed. Traces of dark blue eyeshadow stuck to her eyelids near the lashes. Had she been taking off her makeup when she had the stroke? Or were those blue traces the accretion of years of eyeshadow applied when her eyes glistened like sunlight on dew because love was young and so was she, and applied ever more thickly when love, like the dew, evaporated in the heat of the day? And why blue? Elizabeth wondered. Was that a sublimated longing to have blue eyes, a statement of black inferiority inculcated by a lifetime of Estee Lauder images of the beautiful? Had Andrea worn blue eyeshadow thirty years ago and Elizabeth not noticed? Or had she seen it then, and not believing it a color for brown skin, not seen?

She opened the drawer in the night table next to the bed looking for cotton balls or Q-Tips. Not finding either, she supposed she could have asked a nurse. Instead, she wet her index finger in her mouth and gently rubbed the comatose woman's eyelids until the color was gone.

"I never got used to the tonal variety and richness of his skin color. I never wanted to. As a child I found it magical that I could turn brown by being in the sun. When I first saw black people and found out they were born that way, well . . ." She chuckled aloud. ". . . in my child's mind, black people were magical!"

No one more so than Cal, with his high cheekbones and large dark brown eyes, eyes whose wideness and vulnerability hid behind rose-tinted glasses. He was light-brown-skinned, at least his face was. His chest was another brown, his legs still another.

Once she had compiled a list of all the shades of brown. They had been amazed. There were 140 varieties. Some were obvious: beige, toast, khaki, sorrel, oak. Others were romantic and evocative: sahara, gazelle, Arab, bamboo, deer. Others were exotic and incomprehensible: pablo, badious, kolinsky, cauldron, hopi.

He shared her delight. "I wish Negroes could see their skin color as you see mine."

"Well, if they did, they would have to think about something else that has mystified me for quite a while."

He heard the smile in her voice and answered in kind. "And what might that be?"

"Well, your hands are exposed to sunlight everyday. So, it makes sense that the backs of your hands are darker than your arm. But why does your face stay lighter than your hand? And your penis and ass never see the light, and they're almost black!"

He laughed loudly.

"What shade of brown do you think your penis might be?" She looked at the list. "I don't think it's tallyho brown, do you? No. What about Isabel Brown? Did you ever sleep with an Isabel Brown or an Isabel anybody? Don't answer that. Ah! Ruddle brown! You certainly ruddle me. But I honestly don't know if I can make an accurate assessment without looking at the subject under discussion." She undid his belt, the top button of his trousers, unzipped his pants, and reaching inside the opening of his jockey shorts, grasped his penis, already stiffening in anticipation of her mouth and lips and tongue, and pulled it out . . .

Even now, the years having passed with the lugubriousness of eternity, her eyes were wet with tears, and her vagina moistened more at the memory of a dead man than it ever had with Gregory.

"Time does not heal when past is presence," she said aloud. "Does it, Andrea? You made a career out of being his widow. People see you at a rally, a demonstration or meeting, and they are thrust back into the heroic days of the sixties. They see you and the fabric of time hiding past from present is ripped, and as you stand at the lectern, people hear German shepherd dogs snarling and snapping at black children in the streets of Birmingham. They are standing shoulder to shoulder, one among the quarter million at the Capitol, swaying from side to side, singing 'Black and white together . . . We shall overcome someday'. They see you and fall into the deeper sleep of yesterday's dead hopes and perished dreams.

"Sometimes, when I am feeling bitter and angry and alone, I think his death was the best thing that could have happened for you. It gave your life a purpose, something it had never had. You've done very well making a career as the widow of John Calvin Marshall. You get invited to the White House. You are interviewed on TV when there are racial troubles somewhere. Presidential candidates have their picture taken with you, seeking your endorsement as if it were an imprimatur.

"You're our real Jackie Kennedy because the flesh-and-blood one went on with her life and became Jacqueline Onassis. The nation never forgave her for that. But you became our dowager queen wearing the blood-stained memories of idealism and the hope for a better tomorrow.

"I would look at you on TV and wonder if you were getting any. Have you really gone twenty-five years without sex? More, because you and he didn't have much of a sex life before. And how would I know? The way his body responded to mine told me a lot about how it did not respond to yours."

Elizabeth stopped. "I'm sorry," she said after a moment. "If you were to die at this moment, I would not want those words to be the ones you took into the vacuum of eternity."

Leaning her elbow on the bed, she took one of the woman's hands in hers. "I think I am angry, Andrea, because at least you found *something* to do with your life. While I? I ski." She laughed, harshly, almost maniacally. "That's right. I ski. I have a lovely house on a mountain in Vermont. In fact, I own the mountain. My husband is a dentist in Burlington, and he comes home on weekends. I have my horses and the mountain and in the winter, virgin snow and skis." What if he had lived? Probably nothing would have changed. She would still be living on a mountain in Vermont, grieving, because John Calvin Marshall would not have left his wife for a white woman eleven years his junior.

❖

i had always conceived of history as benign, a patchwork quilt making a beautiful and warm whole. i learned that history is taloned and beaked and lusts for blood.

i remember standing on the steps of the capitol that summer afternoon. almost as far as my eyes could see up that great mall from the capitol to the lincoln memorial were people. blacks. whites. young. old. they had come to demonstrate for freedom. and they had come to hear john calvin marshall.

i had become a messiah, the one who would save them from the old life of sin and initiate them into a new tomorrow of freedom and purity.

but i was only mortal. when i ate the wrong thing my shit smelled just like theirs. why did they not know that? did they honestly think i could save them?

i listened to the cheers and applause and it was all i could do not to walk away. whom were they cheering? it wasn't me. it was john calvin marshall whom they had created in their own image. for an instant, i think i hated them. and myself.

but i did not walk away. i stood there and when the cheering and applause finally stopped, my lips parted and the words poured forth as they always did. there was no thought. speech and thought were indivisible and the two became deed. at those moments, and especially on that particular day, i think i came as close as it is possible for a human being to feel like God, to speak and the word is action. if i had told them to turn and storm the white house fences, they would have done so. but i did not. "I have come here today to plead with the white people of this nation for freedom. But I do not come to plead for freedom for the Negro. No! It is the white man's freedom I seek. Just because you are white and can walk into any restaurant in this nation and be served does not mean you are free. It only means you are privileged, and privilege always exists at the expense of another's degradation. The Negro cannot be free until you stop being white. Only when you stop being white will you stop seeing us as black. Only then will you see that you have been wounded by this disfiguring notion of race more deeply even than we. Freedom can come only when we forgive the wounds inflicted on us by the other — and the ones we've inflicted on ourselves."

they cheered. they applauded. blacks and whites hugged each other and cried and i suppose it did not matter that this moment of utopian euphoria would not last even into the evening. the fact that the moment had existed at all was sufficient. the hope had been created that there could be other moments like it, and maybe somewhere on the backside of history enough of those moments would come together to create a new world.

the next morning the washington post and the new york times praised my speech and speculated that a run for the presidency by me might not succeed but it would certainly make a more honest man out of jfk.

i put down the newspapers slowly. elizabeth and i were having breakfast on the balcony of our suite. it was a clear morning, not too hot yet. i could see in the distance the dome of the capitol. "i am not that man," i said softly. "i am not that man." elizabeth had already read the papers and knew what i was talking about.

"who are you?" she asked quietly.

i shook my head. "i don't know. i don't know."

around nine that evening there was a knock on the door of the suite. elizabeth and i were sitting on the balcony, drinking after dinner coffee and allowing ourselves to be mesmerized by the floodlights playing against the washington monument. the knock at the door startled us. who knew we were there? i had checked into one hotel the night before the march, but elizabeth had arranged for us to go to another one afterward so we could have a rare weekend to ourselves.

she opened the door to see two men in dark suits.

"we're from the bureau, miss adams," one said, holding his identification for her to see. "the director would like to see dr. marshall."

"at this time of night?" i queried, having come into the living room.

"yes, sir."

"give me a moment to get dressed," i responded.

elizabeth followed me into the bedroom. "what's going on?"

i shook my head. "i don't know."

"shall i come with you?"

"no. i'll be all right."

i quickly put on a white shirt, tie and suit and left with the two agents. we went down the service elevator, through the basement and into a car waiting in the alley. they did not want me to be seen anymore than i wanted to be.

i did not bother to ask them what was going on. the director of the bureau did not always share what he knew with presidents, so i knew he wouldn't have told two mere agents why he wanted to see me.

what had happened that would impel the director to want

to see me outside normal business hours? i had been critical of the bureau and its agents more than once for their failure to protect civil rights workers. the director and i had exchanged words in the press over this. why did the director want to see me *now*?

of course. the march. the editorials in the times and the post. john calvin marshall was suddenly a presence, a power to be reckoned with. i wondered if the kennedy brothers were behind this, or if the director was acting on his own.

we reached the justice department quickly and i was taken in a private elevator to the director's office on the fifth floor. the office of the attorney general was also on the floor and i had been there more than once to meet with the younger kennedy brother. was he in there, waiting for the director to tell him how the meeting with me had gone?

i was taken into the outer office. one of the agents knocked on the door of the director's office. a voice within responded. the agent opened the door, motioned me to enter and when i did, pulled it closed behind me.

the director sat behind an enormous desk, and i smiled to myself. the bigger the desk, the smaller the man. he did not rise or smile. he did, indeed, look like a bulldog — the recessed forehead, the heavy cheeks, the squareness of the skull. but a bulldog's eyes were free of malevolence. the director's eyes scintillated with it.

he motioned to the chair on the opposite side of the desk. "i'll get straight to the point, marshall."

he spoke rapidly, the words spilling out of him as if he were afraid their stoppage would reveal his vacuity.

"i have never liked you. i think you are the most dangerous man in america. i think you have misled the negro and stirred up trouble for no reason. you want too much too soon and the white people of this country will never stand for it. if you aren't careful somebody is going to kill you and i say good riddance. i am a patriot, a true american. i love my country and anyone who is a threat to it is my enemy.

"i suppose you read this morning's papers. it must have made you feel mighty important. i wanted to throw up. i don't know what gets into these newspaper people. you make a speech and they want you to be president. this country is not ready for a colored president and the kind of race-mixing you believe in. i listened to that speech of yours yesterday and it made me sick. i said to myself, what if the american people knew about you what i know about you? what would they think then?"

he had a folder in front of him and shoved it across the desk at me.

"what do you think the american people would say if they saw some of those pictures? i've got tapes, too. i'll say this for you: you can make bedsprings squeak."

i opened the folder to see a grainy photograph of a naked elizabeth astride the naked me. beneath it there were more: she with my penis in her mouth, me with my head between her legs, me atop her, me entering her anally.

there was such a welter of emotions: embarrassment, shock and anger and outrage that i had no privacy any more. yet i was also fascinated. we all have photographs of ourselves at picnics, family reunions, weddings, graduations. but we never have the chance to see ourselves making love. part of me wanted elizabeth to see the photos and to reminisce with her about where we had been in this photo and where in that one.

behind the photos was a sheaf of papers, a log of the motels and hotels in which we had made love. i knew we made love a lot but seeing it documented that way, i couldn't help but be impressed.

i closed the folder and looked at the director.
there was a smirk on his face.
"the choice is yours, marshall. if you should suddenly become seriously ill and be unable to keep up your activities in the civil rights arena, then i wouldn't think there would be any reason for the american people to know that you are fucking a white girl almost young enough to be your daughter. quite frankly, i don't care if you fuck a hundred white women. any white woman who prefers a negro to a white man is nothing but trash. good riddance to them. but if you persist, then the washington post, new york times, every columnist, tv station and radio station in america will receive copies of what's in that folder."

i thought about opening the paper one morning to see stories about my relationship with elizabeth and a giddiness swirled inside me unlike any i had known even as a child. my god! i thought. i would be free! i wouldn't have to be john calvin marshall anymore. i could just be . . . be . . . i didn't know what. i could just be.

"well, i suppose you better start licking the stamps," i said to him.

the director turned red. "i don't bluff, marshall!" his voice had taken on an ominous tone.

"i didn't think you did."

he paused. "well, i think i'll send the first copy to your wife."

that stopped me. i had no desire to hurt andrea anymore than she was hurt already. she knew about elizabeth. how could she not? but to see photos, to see names of motels and dates, to hear tapes, that was another matter.

there are moments in all our lives when we must choose the truth of ourselves. such moments are never dramatic. nor can they be seen from the outside. only we know what the moment is calling us to do.

i looked at him. "do you need any help licking the stamps?"

❖

He came back after meeting with the director looking wan. "They know everything about us."

"Everything?" she repeated.

"We can start with the size of my penis and your admiration of it and go from there."

"Oh, God, Cal! What did he say?"

"He said he didn't care if I screwed a hundred white women. The American people were not, however, as understanding. So, unless I withdrew from the civil rights movement, he would make sure the editors of every major paper in the nation received photos of us making love, a tape of our lovemaking, the john calvin marshall fucking hit parade, I guess, and a list of the hotels and motels. I told him that if he wanted some help licking the stamps, I would give him a hand."

"You didn't!"

"Yes, I did!"

Elizabeth shook her head. "I'll leave. That'll make a difference. He can't force you out of the movement. The movement will die without you and he knows it."

"Please don't go. I need you."

Men lie about everything in the world, including "I love you." It is not malicious on their parts or even conscious. The intent is not to hurt or deceive but to protect the fragile heart within. But a man cannot say "I need you" and lie. The admission of his incompleteness, the acknowledgement of his inability to be himself unless you were part of his life was the kind of humility in which the soul could sink roots and a rare love flower. A whimpered and whispered "I need you" was a truth all the roses and boxes of chocolate could never equal.

"And if we pick up the *Washington Post* in the morning and we're on the front page, what will you do?" she asked.

They were sitting on the balcony. Below were the monuments of the nation — the phallus of the Washington Monument, the Lincoln Memorial and the breast-shaped dome of the Capitol. Almost directly below was the White House.

On that hot August night they sat like a normal couple whose lives extended no further than the care and love of each other. It was a moment of delicious illusion that they savored because nothing was normal for them. She was white; he was black. He was 35; she was 24. She was single; he was married. He was a man in whose very body the suffering and aspirations of black history combined to make tangible the soul of a people and the agony of a nation. She was Elizabeth Adams, Lisa to everyone except him. He needed her.

They were seldom alone, except at nights in the tiny rooms of Negro motels in southern towns. She sensed often that it was only because he knew the nights would come that he got through the days of demonstrations and evenings of mass meetings and after those, the staff sessions where he would have to assuage this ego and salve that hurt and parry a challenge to his leadership here and put down open rebellion there. She would sit quietly behind him like an aide at a congressional hearing who produced a document the congressman didn't even know yet that he would need. That was Lisa. Because she was so efficient and unobtrusive at what she did, blacks accepted her — for a while.

Many wondered and others suspected there was more to her relationship with Cal, but in public they were never less than the model of propriety and professionalism. She was the executive assistant who made the plane reservations, rented cars, served as liaison with the local police when Cal went north for fundraisers, answered his critical correspondence, handled speaking engagements and sent cards and gifts in his name to his parents and Andrea on birthdays and anniversaries.

If anyone had dared or cared to see their adjacent rooms with connecting door at motels, it was obvious their relationship was also sexual. She had concluded, however, that people avoid truth because, if they know it, they don't know what they're supposed to do. Truth compels action. A lie maintains the status quo. Regardless of how uncomfortable or even painful the lie, stasis is safety. Truth makes known the unknown. Who needs it?

It would be midnight or 1 A.M. before they got back to the motel. They would sit on the edge of beds with mattresses softened by too many roiling bodies, mattresses smelling of sweat and semen and the thick mucus of vaginas and menstrual blood and moonshine whiskey. Wallpaper hung from the walls in shredded strips as if seared by witnessing too much lust. She would have gotten food, and they balanced paper plates on their laps and ate barbecue ribs, greasy hamburgers, french fries, fried chicken, collard greens, biscuits, cornbread, and drank Coke, beer, moonshine. Never in all those years were they able to go to a restaurant, movie, concert, play or even the park. He was John Calvin Marshall and people believed he could make the blind see and the lame walk.

Sometimes she feared that he hated himself because he couldn't, and she would stroke his naked body with her breasts, slowly, up and down and up, over thighs and buttocks and back, up and down and up until his body shuddered and trembled, and later, sitting astride him, his penis deep within her, she would implore him to thrust deeper and deeper into her until he came and knew himself again as mere flesh and blood and remembered how good that was.

❖

i do not know how it is for white people on a daily basis. i always imagined that hi-story for them was merely backdrop, a muzak heard only when turned up too loud. i imagined that for them hi-story was benign and beneficent, an assumed harmony of which they were only aware when a dissonant chord intruded — the bombing of the world trade center, an economic recession, the assassination of the president.

that is not how it is for blacks, and I suspect, jews. for us, history is, by definition, dissonance. we know history as terror, an omnipresent beast that will devour us if its leash is merely allowed to slacken. history has defined us as its enemy because, by our very beings, we are seen as challenges to its essential premise about order and civilization.

what is that premise? that the essential worth of a human being is determined by his or her race. the tragedy of western civilization is that white people regard themselves as superior because they are born white. the very premise of western civilization — the superiority of the white race — is evil incarnate.

❖

"If the newspapers had made public our relationship, we would have had a chance to be normal. It would have taken a while, but eventually Cal and I would not have had to continue to relinquish privacy in the public sphere.

"I suppose you and I shared that. Were you and he ever able to go to a restaurant, movie, concert, play or even the park together, or walk along a street secure in anonymity? He was John Calvin Marshall. Through television he entered everyone's living room, and because he had, everyone felt they knew him.

"I don't watch much TV anymore. I found myself on constant emotional overload because in the course of an evening I would have fifty relationships, intensely liking this one, disliking that one, wondering what this actor and that actress was like, that politician or that celebrity without portfolio. It is psychically disorienting having powerful emotions about people you know only as images. But television seduces us into trusting image as reality. Daily I watched people approach him. There was always an instant when they realized that all the love and emotion they had for him was not reciprocated, that he had been in their homes and had not known it, that his existence was crucial to their lives while they were nonexistent in his. They had no alternative but to make themselves known to him because they had been forced into a relationship with him.

"He was not allowed a space around himself that no one could enter without permission. But by now television has taken from all of us the space between ourselves and others. It deprives us of the separateness necessary for relationship. If there is no privacy, there is no safety for the soul. If there is no safety for the soul, there is only unrelieved and unrelievable terror.

"I was his privacy, the place of safety for his soul."

On the balcony of the twenty-fifth floor, there was some hint of breeze trying to leaven the moist heat. Cal had taken off his suit coat, removed his tie and unbuttoned the top three buttons of his white shirt, revealing his brown, smooth chest. He slumped in the uncomfortable white-painted wrought iron chair, his legs raised, feet resting on the terrace railing, his head on the back of the chair, hips on the edge. His eyes were closed, as if he were napping. A hand rested lightly on her thigh.

He thought for a moment. "I would live on the side of a mountain and listen to the silence. I would live with the trees and the sky. I would read books and cook gourmet meals and I would love you."

"And what would the silence be like?" she asked, ignoring his declaration of love, disappointed he had felt the need to make it.

"It would be the silence which is the absence of words. It would be the silence which is the absence of presences. It would be the silence that would indicate my release from duty. The silence would be God's declaration that I no longer had to be John Calvin Marshall, that I only had to be who and what *I* wanted to be."

God didn't say that. Cal never told her what the FBI director had done, and only through one of the biographies did she learn that Andrea received the tape, the photographs and the list of dates and motels and room numbers, and, she learned later, so had the *New York Times, Washington Post* and other newspapers and national magazines. Nothing appeared in print.

But those were the days when the media at least still understood the distinction between private and public. Those were the days when a man could act with integrity in the public arena while his private life was a paradigm of immorality. Who could say? Maybe Jack Kennedy would have blown the world to hell in his confrontation with Khrushchev in 1962 if he hadn't been so intent on fucking every woman he could.

Elizabeth trusted a president who was fucking like pussy was going to be banned, because his interest in the continuation of his pleasure would keep his hand away from the nuclear button. If the president was really getting off in bed, then launching nuclear missiles wasn't much of an orgasm. (It had made her wonder if the most important thing to know of a presidential candidate was if he was getting good head from someone. The fate of nations could hinge on whether the head of state was getting blown regularly and properly.)

Americans used to understand that adultery, sexual immorality and perversion had nothing to do with the quality of your work. How many of them were screwing a male lover their wives did not suspect, fondling the hairless vaginas of their daughters, or licking the clitoris of their wife's best friends, while also doing superior work at the office or the factory?

It was sentimental to believe that bad people didn't do good things. The private and public were mutually exclusive realms, and they required vastly different talents and skills. Few lived in both with equal facility. During the presidential primaries of 1988, when Gary Hart was caught with another woman, Lisa had written and told him not to drop out of the race but 'Go for the adultery vote. It's the largest untapped voting bloc in the nation. Don't apologize, dammit! Be proud! Good sex is where you find it, and that ain't always at home.' She never got an answer.

Given how much adultery there was in the country, it seemed that good sex was *seldom* at home. Hart lacked the courage for adultery. Cal didn't. Anyone who permitted himself to be used to further history's ends deserved sympathy and gratitude, not scrutiny of every corner of his private life.

The nights she remembered most were the ones he cried. Some couples had an animal magnetism and you could smell the lust between them. Other couples had an aura of devotion, the sense of belonging together as surely as two parts of hydrogen belonged to one part oxygen to create a unique, life-giving whole. She and Cal were joined by pain. If there was a hurting inside him, she had only to touch him and he would cry.

Often he was unaware of any pain until she put her arms around him in the most ordinary of embraces. He would gasp, and feeling the shudder through his body, she would pull him closer, hold him tightly, merge her body into his. She would take off her clothes and then his so he could feel her breasts against his naked chest, could feel her pubis against his penis, her thighs alongside his, and holding him tightly, she would force the tears up and out and he would cry.

Afterward, when his sobbing subsided, often he would take one of her breasts and suckle like an infant, eyes closed, fingers resting gently at the side of the breast. Sometimes that led to lovemaking. Sometimes he fell asleep, her nipple between his lips.

How many nights he came to her broken by the demands, the needs, the factional infighting, the jealousies, the stubbornness of white southern mayors, the hatreds of white southerners, and toward the end, of blacks, too. How many nights he came wounded by the hands that reached out to touch any part of him, the old black women who came and bent their decrepit bodies to kneel and kiss his hand, the suspension of heartbeats as people received his every word as if each were a drop of plasma restoring life to a blood-depleted body. They called him "The Savior," some to his face with so much hope etched in their voices you thought their hearts would break, some derisively and behind his back. Both shattered him.

Night after night she took the shards and, with her body, made the vessel whole.

APRIL 7, 1964: CLEVELAND, OHIO — REVEREND BRUCE KLUNDER, WHITE, 27, KILLED WHILE PROTESTING THE CONSTRUCTION OF A SEGREGATED SCHOOL. PROTESTORS HAD LAIN DOWN IN FRONT OF A BULLDOZER AT THE CONSTRUCTION. REVEREND KLUNDER HAD LAIN DOWN BEHIND THE BULLDOZER. ATTEMPTING TO AVOID THE PROTESTORS IN FRONT, THE BULLDOZER BACKED UP, CRUSHING REVEREND KLUNDER TO DEATH.

JUNE 21, 1964: PHILADELPHIA, MISSISSIPPI — JAMES CHANEY, 21, ANDREW GOODMAN, 21, AND MICHAEL SCHWERNER, 25, MURDERED.

JULY 11, 1964: COLBERT, GEORGIA — LT. COL. LEMUEL PENN, 49, MURDERED WHILE RETURNING FROM TWO WEEKS OF ARMY RESERVE TRAINING BY KLANSMEN WHO WANTED "TO KILL A NIGGER."

JULY 12, 1964: MEADVILLE, MISSISSIPPI — A MAN FISHING IN THE MISSISSIPPI RIVER FINDS LOWER HALF OF BADLY DECOMPOSED BODY. THE FOLLOWING DAY A SECOND BODY IS FOUND, DECAPITATED, A PIECE OF WIRE WRAPPED AROUND ITS TORSO. CHARLES EDDIE MOORE, 20, AND HENRY DEE, 19, HAD BEEN MURDERED BY KLANSMEN WHO BELIEVED THE TWO WERE BLACK MUSLIMS PLANNING AN ARMED UPRISING. ALTHOUGH THE TWO MURDERERS CONFESSED, ALL CHARGES WERE DISMISSED WITHOUT EXPLANA- TION.

FEBRUARY 26, 1965: MARION, ALABAMA — JIMMIE LEE JACKSON, 27, KILLED BY A STATE TROOPER DURING A CIVIL RIGHTS MARCH.

MARCH 11, 1965: SELMA, ALABAMA — REVEREND JAMES REEB, A WHITE, UNITARIAN MINISTER FROM BOSTON, BEATEN ON THE STREETS OF SELMA AND DIES TWO DAYS LATER. IN CONTRAST TO THE MURDER OF JIMMIE LEE JACKSON, REEB'S DEATH PROVOKES NATIONAL OUTRAGE. PRESIDENT JOHNSON PHONES REEB'S WIDOW

AND VICE-PRESIDENT HUMPHREY ATTENDS HIS FUNERAL. JIMMIE LEE JACKSON'S MOTHER RECEIVED NO PHONE CALL FROM THE PRESIDENT AND NO PRESIDENTIAL REPRESENTATIVE ATTENDED HIS FUNERAL. FOUR DAYS AFTER REEB'S DEATH, PRESIDENT JOHNSON SENDS A VOTING RIGHTS BILL TO CONGRESS AND ADDRESSES THE NATION ON TELEVISION, CONCLUDING WITH THE WORDS, "WE SHALL OVER-COME."

MARCH 25, 1965: LOWNDES COUNTY, ALABAMA — VIOLA LIUZZO, 40, A WHITE MOTHER OF FIVE FROM DETROIT, SHOT AND KILLED WHILE DRIVING A CIVIL RIGHTS MARCHER BACK TO SELMA AFTER THE SELMA-MONTGOMERY MARCH.

JUNE 2, 1965: VARNADO, LOUISIANA — ONEAL MOORE, 34, FIRST BLACK DEPUTY IN WASHINGTON PARISH, SHOT AND KILLED.

JULY 18, 1965: ANNISTON, ALABAMA — WILLIE BREWSTER, 39, SHOT AND KILLED WHILE DRIVING HOME FROM THE PIPE FOUNDRY WHERE HE WORKED.

AUGUST 20, 1965: HAYNEVILLE, ALABAMA — JONATHAN DANIELS, 26, A WHITE MINISTERIAL STUDENT, SHOT AND KILLED.

JANUARY 3, 1966: TUSKEGEE, ALABAMA — SAMUEL YOUNGE, JR., 22, A STUDENT CIVIL RIGHTS ACTIVIST, SHOT AND KILLED TRYING TO USE WHITES ONLY RESTROOM AT A SERVICE STATION.

JANUARY 10, 1966: HATTIESBURG, MISSISSIPPI — VERNON DAHMER, 58, VOTING RIGHTS ACTIVIST, KILLED WHEN HIS HOME IS BOMBED.

JUNE 10, 1966: NATCHEZ, MISSISSIPPI — BEN CHESTER WHITE, 67, MURDERED BY THREE WHITE MEN WHO WANTED TO KILL A NIGGER.

FEBRUARY 27, 1967: NATCHEZ, MISSISSIPPI — WHARLEST JACKSON, 37, MURDERED AFTER BEING PROMOTED TO A PREVIOUSLY WHITE-

AND ALL OUR WOUNDS FORGIVEN

ONLY JOB AT THE ARMSTRONG RUBBER COMPANY WHERE HE
WORKED.

MAY 12, 1967: JACKSON, MISSISSIPPI — BENJAMIN BROWN, 22,
WHILE GOING TO A RESTAURANT TO GET A SANDWICH FOR HIS WIFE,
KILLED WHEN POLICE FIRE ON PROTESTORS THROWING ROCKS AND
BOTTLES FARTHER DOWN THE THE SAME STREET.

FEBRUARY 8, 1968: ORANGEBURG, SOUTH CAROLINA — SAMUEL
HAMMOND, 19, DELANO MIDDLETON, 18, HENRY SMITH, 20,
SHOT AND KILLED WHEN HIGHWAY PATROLMEN FIRE ON STUDENT
PROTESTORS.

❖

i have wondered if the real work of the civil rights movement
was not interracial sex. do not misunderstand. i am not
deriding the passage of the 1964 civil rights act or the 1965
voting rights act. i am not dishonoring the memories of all
of us who died. but if social change is the transformation of
values, then the civil rights movement did not fulfill itself.
there has not been any diminution in the ethic of white
supremacy. instead racism has added legions of *black* ad-
herents, making america an integrated society in a way i
never dreamed. our racial suspicions and hatreds have
made us one nation.

the sixties were unique because so many blacks and so
many whites took the risk of extending themselves toward
the other. in the twentieth century, there was a brief period
of a mere eight years when a significant number of blacks
and whites lived and worked and slept with each other. those
who did so were forever changed.

i used to feel guilty about what seemed a compulsion to be with a white woman. i do not know even now when the feeling began. i suspect it antedates my existence, that it begins — where? — on the slave auction block at annapolis? or charleston? or savannah? who was that african who survived the middle passage, survived the breaking-in period in the west indies where he was acculturated to slavery and then, brought to these shores and placed on an auction block? while standing there did he look out and see for the first time a woman with skin the color of death and hair the color of pain and eyes the color of the corpse-filled sea? did he look at her and she look at him and know?

i was around 7. one saturday morning i went into montgomery with my father. we were walking along a street. i happened to look up and see a white girl on the other side. she looked like a woman. given my age, she was probably no more than 12. into my mind came the words: "i'm going to marry her one day." she did not see me, did not know i existed on the planet. what did i *see* that led to such words? it was as if the story had been leading to that moment for centuries: "i'm going to marry her one day."

that is how social change happens. a 7-year-old alabama colored boy thinks a thought it is doubtful any other 7-year-old alabama colored boy had ever thought. except, and i need to be accurate, i didn't think it. the thought thought me. however, i did not reject it. other 7-year-old alabama colored boys had been thought by similar thoughts — 'i wish i could marry her." "i sure would like to marry her." they yearned. i asserted: "i'm going to marry her one day."

what did it mean? what was i trying to tell myself?

the first time elizabeth and i were together. we were both nervous. more. we were frightened. she was a virgin, but the anxiety was other. what we were about to do had been forbidden for centuries. black man. white woman. it was a social taboo with almost as much force as the one against incest. black men were killed if a white man thought they might be thinking about white women. Emmett Till. Mack Charles Parker.

could she and i act as individuals? were we strong enough to defy four centuries of history?

in the sixties a lot of black men and white women tried to heal history with their bodies. i am not naive. i know many of those black men and white women abused each other. i know many black women were made to feel worthless as they saw black men walk past them to get to the nearest white woman. history extracts its price, regardless. i also know that some of history's wounds could not have been tended any other way.

i loved her from the moment i saw her picture on the front page of the newspaper. who was this young white girl that dared cross over, this young woman whose beauty was apparent even in the grainy texture of a newspaper photo, this young woman whose wealth and background exempted her from the cares and concerns of ninety-nine percent of those on the planet? was she guilt-ridden because she was white and wealthy? that evening on huntley-brinkley they showed film of the arrests in nashville and there she was, walking easily, almost leisurely, from the store where they had been sitting-in and into the paddy wagon.

andrea noticed and said: she's quite lovely, isn't she?

embarrassed, i wanted to demur but i sensed it was important not to betray myself — and her: yes. she is.

neither andrea or i could escape the reverence in my tone.

a few weeks later when the invitation came from fisk, i accepted immediately and asked andrea to come with me, which was unusual. she never accompanied me on my travels, not even in those early years. two years later, when i returned from california with elizabeth, i think she was relieved that someone was finally going to take responsibility for my aloneness.

that phelps girl is at fisk. i don't think i want to be there when you meet her.

i tried to deny that my eagerness to go to fisk was to meet elizabeth. i was confused. i did not understand why i needed to meet her. i knew it appeared to andrea to be a sexual attraction. it was not. i could've hidden that because it is essentially meaningless except if personal gratification is the essence of one's existence. perhaps i wanted andrea there to protect me. i thought if she was with me, nothing would happen and i would be safe.

after lunch at the fisk president's house, andrea and i got in the car to drive back to atlanta. we were both afraid to break the silence, afraid that any word would mean the end of the marriage. yet, if the silence continued for too long, that, too, would mean the end. i did not know what to say. there was nothing to say.

elizabeth.

i had said her name like a lover consenting to go wherever the beloved led.

andrea: listen and don't respond. if you say anything, it will be a lie, and i don't like you when you lie. you can't help it. you're a man. truths of the heart confuse men. they confuse women, too, but we know it is better to speak them aloud. men lie aloud and speak the truth to themselves. women speak the truth aloud but believe the lies they tell themselves.

we fear truths of the heart because, more often than not, they hurt. they complicate our lives. but that is only appearance. ultimately, truths of the heart simplify, even if we aren't able to always believe them.

i do not like being the wife of john calvin marshall. i did not say that i do not love you. i love you more now than the afternoon we met my freshman year. i love the man you are becoming. i love you for choosing to be the leader of our people. i love you, john calvin. being your wife is another matter.

i do not like the tightness in my stomach everytime a car passes the house. i do not like the dread of waiting for the next window to shatter from a rock or implode from the blast of a shotgun. i do not like the memory of the house falling around me; i do not like thinking, what if i had not taken three steps toward the kitchen? i would have been killed. i do not like to hear the phone ring when you're away because one time i will pick it up and someone will tell me you are dead.

most of all, i do not like that i am married to you and you are not married to me. i looked at that girl today and i envied the look in her eyes. i don't mean when we were standing in the foyer but before you spoke. i noticed your eyes look up into the balcony and i knew you had found her. i turned and looked. i expected to see hero worship in her eyes. i expected to see the thick glow of infatuation. instead i was shocked. on her face, in her eyes, i saw a look of understanding. it's not fair, i thought. i have tried so hard to be what you need. you have scarcely noticed because my efforts have been so far off the mark. you and she had not even exchanged a word, and yet, she seemed to know you in ways i never will. and afterward, in the foyer, did you notice that she stood and waited for you to come to her? did you notice that?

john calvin: yes, i did.

andrea: thanks for not lying. seeing how she was with you was remarkable. god, i hated her. i really hated her. it is not possible for a black woman to move through the world with such assurance, such self-confidence. how old is she? 19? my god! there has not been a 19-year-old black girl in the history of western civilization who could stand on the earth as if it were her unquestioned possession. but, i can't hate her. it's not her fault. and, this is what i want you to know. it is not yours, either. black men. white women. history has decreed that the two belong to each other in ways that black men and black women, white men and white women cannot. thank you for asking me to come. having seen the two of you together, having heard you speak her name, i will know that this is not some sexual fling. no woman likes to be rejected for that which all women have — pussy, if you will excuse me. if your husband is going to be sharing himself with another woman, at least let it be for something he could not have with you. i don't know if that will lessen the hurt, but it will keep the hysteria within manageable boundaries — some of the time. it will assuage the loneliness — some of the time. it does not mean i forgive you — yet. it does not mean that i do not hate her. but my mind understands. some day, if i am blessed, my heart will accept.

i said nothing but when we got home, we made love more truly and more tenderly than we ever had and ever would again.

late that night, when i was downstairs going over my notes for the next day's classes, i could hear her, upstairs, crying.

CARD

it seemed logical that the young would respond eagerly to my calls for social change. i did not understand that for the young change has no other content than change. the appearance of activity differentiates them from their parents. the task of youth is this definitive act of differentiation because the young can have only one priority — to see themselves.

i mistook their eagerness to follow me as confirmation. but ardor is as characteristic of youth as the large, moist eyes of cocker spaniels. though that ardor combined with courage to create a movement that ended racial segregation, what a price the nation extracted from its young to pay a debt they had not incurred.

but did i have an alternative? the foundation of national policy for resolving racial conflict was set by brown v. board of education. the supreme court required children to do what adults had not — desegregate the nation.

it seemed logical. the young were less imbued with prejudice. because they were young they could more readily learn and live an ethic of social equality. but we robbed them of childhood and thus of integrity.

they never knew. adults are skillful at pandering to youth. listen to the platitudes of any high school or college commencement address. the young are flattered into believing that the responsibility for the future of humanity is now passing into their hands. they are told that they are the best and the brightest, the most caring and sensitive youth to ever tread the crust of mother earth. they applaud with self-congratulatory fervor when they are told that their generation must and will succeed where their parents' generation has failed.

thus we lie to the young in america. we leave it to them to discover, with a shock, that youth is the shortest and most fleeting period of their lives, that the living will get more arduous as they age, and that the hallmark of maturity is the courage to withstand uncertainty and paradox and the absence of a solution for anything, anything at all.

1974

The phone woke him.

He opened his eyes to narrow slits and peered across the floor at the clock radio whose luminous numbers shone like evil contemplating itself.

Bobby knew he should let the phone ring until whoever it was hung up or died. In the history of the world nobody had ever received good news at 4 A.M.

"The phone's ringing," came a sleepy female voice from the other side of the mattress.

"Don't you think I know that," he growled, wondering who the bitch was. "If you care so damn much, answer the muthafucka your damn self!" He laughed harshly. "Bitch!" he added, as if he had left the sentence incomplete.

He leaned over and snatched the receiver off the phone

from where it sat on the floor next to the radio. "What the fuck you want?"

He heard a sigh, followed by a soft chuckle.

"Bitch!" he screamed. "If you want to sigh, come on over! I got something between my legs that'll make you do more than sigh, goddammit!"

"You get more charming with the years," came the calm response in a soft female voice.

Card was silent for a moment and then recognized who it was. "Shit!"

"It's so nice to be remembered," the voice said sweetly.

"What the fuck do you want?" he said with a cold fury, sitting up now, grasping the receiver so tightly his hand hurt. "Do you know what the fuck time it is? And no, the check is not in the mail."

The voice laughed genuinely, and in spite of himself, Card smiled. "Guess you knew that, huh?" he responded, calmer now.

"I wouldn't expect you to break a four-year habit."

"At least I'm consistent."

"When one is devoid of virtues, consistency is all that remains."

"Goddammit, Kathy!" he flared.

"I apologize, Bobby."

"Fine! Now, get to the fucking point."

It had been eternities since he had heard that voice as seductive as promises, and he was frightened that it could still make him want to reach for what he had been unable to grasp.

He waited in the darkness for her to speak and became wary as the silence merged with the darkness and she hid within one or the other or behind both, a snake burrowed in the ground sensing the prey oblivious to its imminent death.

Just as his impatience was about to explode, she said softly, "Bobby?"

"Dammit, you know my name and I know my name. What the fuck is it? Something happen to Adisa?" he asked, the thought occurring to him for the first time.

"Bobby?" she repeated, her voice hesitant and seeming to break like scraps of cloud. "It's George. He's dead."

"George?" he echoed reflexively, not knowing who she was talking about.

"He shot himself."

"Shot himself!" and he saw a thin face with a wisp of beard. "George!" he exclaimed, his body suddenly rigid. "George shot himself?" Then he chuckled, shaking his head nervously. "You got to be kidding, Kathy. George wouldn't do that."

"That's what I thought. But he did."

Card shook his head again. "Uh-uh. That's not possible."

"Wylie just called and told me. He wanted me to get in touch with you."

"What the fuck for?" he shot back, suddenly surly again.

Kathy chuckled. "That's what I wanted to ask him."

"He think I give a fuck about George blowing his brains out," he continued, not having heard Kathy's quiet riposte.

"Yes, but he doesn't know you as well as I do."

"Fuck you, too!"

"Wylie wanted me to ask you to come to the funeral. He needs you."

"Fuck that! I went to my last funeral when Cal got blown away. Tell Wylie I'm sorry."

"You call him and tell him. Sorry I had to wake you. Now, tell me. What sixteen-year-old white girl are you in bed with tonight? Or have you matured to seventeen-year-olds?"

Card looked guiltily at the mass of blond hair spilling over the top of the sheet. "Anything else on your mind?" he asked Kathy.

"Well, since you asked, shall I tell Adisa that her father said hello and that he loves her?"

"Tell her whatever the fuck you want to!" He slammed down the receiver and fell back onto the bed, fists clenched.

"Sounded like bad news," a voice said sympathetically from the other side of the mattress.

"Goddammit!" Card spluttered, leaping from the mattress and rushing across the room to turn on the light switch next to the door. "Who the fuck are you?" he screamed at the pudgy face of the girl clutching the sheet in front of her pale naked body. "Who the fuck asked you anything, and what the fuck are you doing here anyway?" Card hurried over and tore the sheet from her hands, flinging it toward the foot of the mattress.

The girl, her blue eyes wide with fear, didn't look to be more than sixteen. She cringed at the head of the mattress, her back against the wall, arms crossed over her breasts as her eyes filled with tears.

Card laughed harshly as he stared down at her. "You oughta cover 'em up! Don't understand why somebody as young as you should have tits drooping like an old lady's. Get the fuck outta here! Go on back to Brooklyn or Queens or Teaneck and tell your girl friends that you fucked a nigger and it's going to be the highlight of your sorry ass life." He drew back his arm as if to strike her, then let it drop. "Didn't you hear me? Get the fuck OUT!"

The girl leaped from the mattress, picking up her clothes from the floor. Card shoved her across the room, grabbed her shorts, underpants and tanktop and threw them at her. "Put 'em on in the goddam hall! Just get out of my sight!"

The girl scooped up her garments and, clutching them to her breasts, ran from the apartment, sobbing. Card slammed the door behind her, then, leaning against it, trembled. In the hallway he heard the rustle of clothes being put on hastily, the gasps of inhaled sobs and sniffling, then the sound of running steps down the hallway and the stairs. He went to the window, raised the shade and looked down in time to see her running west on Twelfth Street toward Avenue A. "Bitch," he said softly.

He fell down on the mattress and stared at the blank wall across the small room, a mad glint in his eyes, jaw rigid and fists balled, the nails digging into the palms of his hands.

"Fuck you, muthafucka! Fuck you!"

Once Bobby Card had been thin and lean as winter. Now his stomach was flabby and soft, and where there had been tempered muscles in his shoulders, arms and legs, there was only flesh. He stared at the wall from dark eyes sunk deeply between a protruding forehead and high cheekbones. His shaven head completed the impression of someone whose face was more skeletal than human.

Though his tiny eyes stared at the wall, they were not seeing it. Nor were they seeing some inner landscape or replaying a drama from his 32 years. They saw nothing and as long as they did, he could remain still; the rage would pass and he wouldn't have to go back to the hospital. He had pills somewhere, but even in the hospital he hadn't liked to take them. White people had a pill for everything. If you were angry, they had a pill that left you floating somewhere. If they thought you had floated too far away, they had a pill to make you feel like green grass in the summer time. Honkeys could cut off your balls and leave you thinking you were the biggest stud east of the Mississippi.

"Fuck you, muthafucka!" He said it less loudly and less vehemently this time. "Fuck you," he repeated, his voice barely a whisper.

He heard the noise of a car horn from the street.

"Fuck you, too," he said and gave a high-pitched cackle.

He noticed the light coming through the window and got

up and raised the shade on the other. By ten o'clock the heat in the one-room apartment on the fourth floor would be unbearable and he would go downstairs and sit on the stoop with the winos and drink Coca-Cola. (It was funny how the winos admired him for going to AA while they unscrewed the cap of another bottle of Thunderbird.) Or, maybe he'd go over to Washington Square and jive some little white girl looking for summer adventure.

He shook his head, remembering the girl he'd found in his bed an hour ago. Card assumed he'd picked her up from the bookstore in the Village where he worked from six until midnight. There were always bitches coming in who assumed anybody black sitting behind the cash register at a bookstore in Greenwich Village had to be a poet. Some white bitches were funny like that. They'd give pussy in a minute to somebody they thought was a writer or a poet and wouldn't give shit to a football player.

"I write poetry with my dick," he liked to tell them, and the bitches would blush and he could smell their panties getting wet, and see it if they were wearing tight shorts.

He must have brought the bitch home from the bookstore, or maybe he found her sitting on a bench in the park smoking a reefer. But he couldn't remember and that wasn't like him. He never asked their names. Bitch was good enough. But this was the first time he had woken up *surprised* to find a bitch in bed. His memory had been better than that when he had stayed drunk all the time.

Without bothering to put on anything, Card walked out of the room and down the hallway to the john. A couple of years ago some old Puerto Rican broad with a mole the size of a marble in the crease next to her right nostril and hair growing out of her ears who went around with rosary beads in her hands all the time had complained to the landlord about Card's habit of walking naked down the hallway to the bathroom. What the fuck did it matter to her? It didn't make sense to put on pants to go to the bathroom because he would just have to pull them down when he got there. Landlord had told her to call the police, and the bitch had done it. He had sweet-talked them, and they were scarcely out of the building before he was banging on the bitch's door. He smiled at the memory of her opening it to see his .22 pointing at one of her watery eyes. And before she could scream he had pulled the trigger. CLICK! The gun was empty, but she hadn't known that. He chuckled. Bitch shit in her panties because he smelled it. She had moved out the next day. Probably went back to Puerto Rico where she belonged. If you weren't ready for anything and everything, keep your ass out of New York.

He returned to the apartment, slamming the door behind him. "Wake up, muthafuckas!" he yelled and then laughed.

He went to the kitchen sink and stood for a moment trying to decide whether to wash his face or brush his teeth first. Every morning it was the same damn decision. After all these years he should've decided one way or the other. But, dammit, every day was different. Some days he woke up and was ready to take on the world. On days like that he brushed his teeth first. Other days he wanted to glide along the streets unnoticed, as much as a bald-headed nigger could who looked like death. Those days he washed his face first. Then there were the days he didn't give a shit one way or the other. That was most of them. He needed two or three cans of Coke and half a pack of cigarettes just to wake up. Those used to be the days he would do something crazy. He hadn't had one of those in a while.

He took the bar of soap from the piece of plywood covering the bathtub. George had never accustomed himself to how seriously Card took face washing.

"Nigger, it don't matter how much you rub. You ain't gon'

be white when you get through. The dirt comes off but the nigger just gets rubbed in deeper." Card had never responded or hurried, especially back in those days.

He soaped his hands until the lather dripped from them, then applied it slowly, working it with his fingertips around his nostrils, his ears, over and around the cheekbones, beneath his chin. Then, taking the washcloth from where it hung off the side of the plywood, he wet it, squeezed out the water, and wiped the lather from his face. He repeated the process several times before patting his face dry with paper towels.

There was a lot of shit George never understood; waking up was one. "Black folks could be free, Card, and you still washing your goddam face."

"Niggers ain't never gon' be free, George, so I might as well be clean."

Card frowned. "And I'm still here, muthafucka, and you ain't."

He brushed his teeth, then walked across the room and picked up his underwear, jeans and T-shirt from the floor. As he slipped them on, he was vaguely aware that they might be dirty and smelly. So what?

He made the bed neatly. Even if it was only a mattress on the floor, it had to be impeccably made each morning. He might look like his clothes came from the Salvation Army, and sometimes they did, but women didn't care about shit like that. However nothing turned a bitch off more than a man's unmade bed. It got her to thinking about who might have been there the night before, and every bitch needed the illusion that she was Miss One and Only and Forever, even if she didn't want to be.

When he finished, he picked up the crumpled, half-filled pack of cigarettes off the floor, lit one and sat down on the mattress, the only piece of furniture in the room. He looked around as if searching for something to look at. There was nothing. The walls were painted a shade of green nature would have rejected. The green was peeling to reveal a layer of white paint beneath and who knew how many layers and what colors beneath that. His few clothes were on hangers on a nail on the back of the door. Next to the door was the sink, bathtub, a tiny refrigerator on top of which was a two-burner gas stove he never used.

He looked as if seeing the room for the first time. He tried to remember how long he had lived there. At least two years, he thought. Maybe more. He had moved in after his last hospital stay and that had been more than two years ago. Right, he remembered. Four years ago because that was the last time he had seen or talked to Kathy until that morning.

Card got up, went to the window, raised it and flicked the cigarette out. He turned back into the room, looked down at himself, at the wrinkled T-shirt and rumpled pants. After a moment's hesitation, he stripped, went across the room and took the plywood board from the bathtub and turned on the faucets. While the tub was filling with a slow and tepid trickle of water, he turned on the radio in time to hear the five-thirty newscast.

He knew there would be nothing about George on it, but a man who had been the second-best organizer in the civil rights movement wasn't supposed to be just another dead nigger.

Card chuckled, and it was as if he could hear George saying, "What do you mean, 'second-best organizer?' " It had been a joke between them, because Card had been the best and George knew it. But the two of them together had been something to see, Card recalled with pride.

He turned off the water, climbed into the tub and bathed quickly. He found a half-dirty towel in a cabinet beneath the sink and dried himself. He shaved and then took a pair of lightweight brown slacks and a pink shirt from the hangers on the back of the door and dressed. Shoving his feet into his sandals, he took his wallet and keys from the jeans lying on the floor, took a look around the room and left.

The street was quiet. The only person out was the old Italian man sitting on a folding chair in front of the mortuary. He looked like a corpse waiting for the casket to come.

"Buon giorno, Signor Ghiraldi," Card called, waving.

The old man looked up, smiled and waved. "Whadda you say, Card?" he answered in a voice stronger than his frail body should've been able to hold.

Card held out his arms and shrugged. "It's going to be another hot one."

"Whadda you 'spect? It's summer."

Card laughed, waved and continued down the block. He smiled. He still did automatically the things a good organizer was supposed to do. He doubted if there was a person on the block he didn't know, at least to speak to. Ten years ago he could've gone to any town in the South and by sundown been able to tell you who held the power, how they used it and what he would have to do to get them to use it to get Negroes some freedom.

He crossed Avenue A and continued on to First Avenue where the uptown traffic was beginning to build toward the morning rush hour. He continued a block up First Avenue to a nondescript diner in the middle of the block.

"What's happening, Maureen?" he said to the dark-haired woman behind the counter.

"You sick?" she smiled. "Haven't seen you in here this early in a while, Card."

"Thought I'd come in early and make your day," he laughed, strolling to the back of the diner and sliding into the last booth where he could look out on to the avenue. It was a typical New York diner, with a counter and stools running the length of the room and booths along the windows. He felt more at home there than in his apartment. He ate there everyday. The food was adequate, if plain, and the servings were almost more than he could eat, and his appetite was not small.

"Coffee?"

"Who made it? You or Patrick?"

A husky man with dirty gray hair and a white apron covering the lower part of his body stepped out of the kitchen behind Card. "You don't like my coffee?" he asked. "That's what's wrong with you coloreds. You got no taste."

"If I had taste, honky, I wouldn't eat here. What I want to know, Pat, is when are you going to die and let Maureen put some class in this roach trap."

"I can't do that, Card. If I die you'll marry her and I couldn't rest easy in my grave knowing my own sister was married to a colored."

They laughed.

"You having the usual?"

Card nodded. He settled back in the booth and smiled. It was good having a place where nobody wanted anything from you except that you be well. There'd been weeks when Pat had carried him on a tab, and Card had always paid him back — and with a little extra. Sometimes when Card came in the afternoon, he'd help out in the kitchen to give Pat a half hour or so to sit down and smoke a cigarette.

Maureen brought two cups of coffee to the booth and slid in opposite Card. She took a pack of cigarettes from the pocket of her beige uniform, shook two out, lit them and handed one to Card.

"It's going to be hotter 'n hell today," she said.

"Least you'll be in here with the air conditioning."

She shrugged. "Another hour and this place will fill up and from then until three or so, I'll be running back and forth. The sweat'll be coming off me like I was outside."

Card took a sip of coffee and nodded. It was a conversation they'd had last summer, the one before that, and the one before that. The familiarity of routine and habit were probably the most security one could ask for in this world.

He looked at her as he dragged deeply on the cigarette. She was his age, maybe a little older. She had probably been pretty once, pretty in that way of open innocence which seemed peculiar to Irish Catholic girls in their plaid school uniforms. Now she was just plain, with tiny wrinkles beginning to spread out from her blue eyes. Her short dark hair was not styled but simply lay on her head as if resigned to the superiority of an unknown foe.

"How you been?" he wanted to know.

She shrugged. "What can I tell you?"

He nodded. Her life wouldn't change and they both knew it. She got up at three-thirty every morning, drove across the Queensboro Bridge with Pat, helped him set up in the kitchen, unlocked the door at six, closed up at seven in the evening, back across the bridge and in bed by nine. Card knew her husband had been killed in 'Nam, that her mother had died a few months later and she had moved back home to help Pat for a few months and the months had become years and the years a life.

"You?"

"Same ol' same ol'."

They sat quietly, smoking and drinking coffee. Maureen left for a few moments to talk to the two waitresses when they reported for work and then returned. Pat came out of the kitchen, put a plate of two eggs over easy, toast and hash browns in front of Card.

"Looks good, Pat," Card said.

Pat shook his head. "You getting old, Card. You said something nice."

They laughed.

Pat slapped him on the shoulder and returned to the kitchen. "You OK?" Maureen asked, after a moment. "You're quiet this morning."

He shrugged, chewing slowly.

"I'm not prying or anything, but, are you OK?"

"Hell, how should I know?"

Maureen smiled wistfully. "Yeah. You know, sometimes I'm glad I don't have time to think. If I did, who knows what I might find? You know?"

He nodded.

"I mean, if I'd thought when I was a kid going to St. Joseph's every morning that this is what my life was going to be like, I don't know what I would've done. You know?"

He nodded again. "What did you want to be when you were a kid?"

"You mean after I got over wanting to be a nun?" she laughed. "I don't know. It was all kind of vague. Secretary, I guess. The one thing I was sure of was that I'd have a house and kids and who knows? Maybe even a white picket fence." She frowned. "Pat has been after me to get the hell out. It has been eight years now since Michael was killed. I suppose I might have taken what the army gave me and the survivor's benefits and moved somewhere, started over. But then, mother died three months after Michael. Between Christmas and Easter I became a widow and an orphan. I never knew my dad. He was killed in the Second World War. By the time I came out of shock after Michael and mother, I had already moved back into the house to help Pat and that was that. But, to tell the truth, it never occurred to me to move anywhere. Isn't that sad, Card? Never crossed my mind. Where the hell would I have gone? And to do what? I didn't have any skills and I'm nobody's pinup girl." She shrugged. "What the hell? At least here, I got friends. People like you.

I got a place. Something to do. But you've heard all that more than once."

Carl nodded. "Maybe a friend is somebody who listens as many times as you need to say it."

Maureen smiled. "So, what about you? What did you want to be when you grew up?"

He ate quietly, as if he hadn't heard, but he had and she knew. He thought about the dusty roads that went through the colored section of Willert, Mississippi, and the little boy who had played baseball with tin cans and sticks on those silent roads and the white men who came in the night looking for their lives on the bodies of black women and the threat to his if he saw what he was not supposed to see, heard what he was not supposed to hear and said what no one would listen to, and he looked up at Maureen and said simply, "Alive."

He finished the last of the hash browns, pushed the plate to the side, took another of Maureen's cigarettes, lit it and repeated, "Alive."

It was a little after seven when he left the diner, giving Maureen a hug and warm kiss on the cheek, and got on the Fourteenth-Street crosstown bus. It was not time yet for the bus to be crowded, and he had the long backseat to himself. After all those years of *having* to sit in the back of the bus, he still sat there when he had a choice. What you chose didn't matter when it was your choice.

He stared idly through the window at the people walking along the street. He'd never understood why New Yorkers looked as tired at seven in the morning going to work as they would at six coming home. They hurried along but there was no spring, no liveliness in their steps. They walked as if the weight of the skyscrapers was a heaviness in their souls.

Card left the bus at Seventh Avenue and took the IRT local uptown. He had plenty of time. Amy didn't leave for work until eight-thirty, he recalled. He didn't know why he assumed she was living in the same place. Maybe she had gotten married and moved to the East Side or out of the city altogether. He didn't think so.

They had lived together — on and off — for six years. He had put her through a lot — the two nervous breakdowns, having a child by another woman, the drinking. And here he came again. This time he didn't know why.

He got off the subway at Seventy-second and Broadway, walked the long block over to West End Avenue and continued north. It was cool, almost chilly in the dark morning shadows of the apartment buildings. Back in the mid-sixties he'd gone to a "movement" fund-raising party at Harry Belafonte's apartment, which was somewhere on West End. He didn't remember much about it except that Lena Horne had been there and he'd told her that he'd eat a mile of her shit just to see where it came from and she'd wrinkled her nose, smiled coldly, and said, "I take it you're a gourmet."

He had met Amy at a fund-raising party after Cal got him out of Shiloh. Those were the days when whities loved niggers because they were nonviolent and didn't mind getting their asses kicked and their heads cracked and their hearts shot out. Some rich whitey would call up his rich whitey friends and organize a party in his big apartment on West End Avenue, Central Park West or some damn street where more black poodles lived than niggers. They all wanted John Calvin Marshall to be there but Cal wouldn't go near one of the fund-raisers unless there was a guarantee of a million dollars being raised. Of course, Cal never said that. Lisa handled those negotiations. Rich whiteys knew how to talk to each other.

He had been astonished to find himself in the same room with white people, white people who spoke to him with respect, white people who admired him. It was a while before he experienced their admiration as little different than that lavished on a dancing bear, or a lion trained to go against instinct and leap through a flaming hoop. He was the Mississippi colored boy who grew up without running water or indoor toilet, the eighth of thirteen children who had been taken out of school in March each year to plant cotton and didn't return until after the cotton scrapings were picked in November. Yet, he had persevered and learned to read and write, had finished high school and gone to Fisk University for a year before dropping out to work with John Calvin Marshall.

It took him a while to understand that white people cared only that his presence absolved them of guilt for the poverty he had overcome. He was Exhibit A for the defense. "Look how much he has become like us. If the rest of you niggers don't, it's your own damn fault, which means it is our duty and obligation to continue kicking your black butts as hard as we can."

The anger had already begun when he met Amy. Her father was a lawyer, a close friend and advisor of Cal's and a good political strategist. He was one of the few white people Card liked and respected, though he doubted Paul had any affection or respect for him anymore.

The party had been at Paul's brownstone in the Village on a narrow, quiet street where all the buildings had heavy oak doors and brass knockers. She opened the door and for the first time in his life he felt he was not alone and was not surprised when her first words were, "I'm really sorry you have to go through something like this. I hope it won't be too much of a drag."

She was a little shorter than his five feet, nine inches, with curly black hair crowning her oval face. Her complexion was swarthy and Card wondered if there was a nigger somewhere in the woodpile. He learned later that there were Russian Jewish ancestors "who lived near the Black Sea." That night, though, standing in the doorway, he had been more immediately aware of her sturdiness, and that was the word that had come to him then. She stood there as solid as the oak door. Separately, her features were not attractive — the mouth was wide, too wide for a white girl, the nose was thick, and the eyes large but devoid of innocence. The body was heavy, an impression created more by a large bone structure than fat, though the breasts seemed large behind the peach-colored blouse and the hips wide beneath the black skirt. Yet, the sum overwhelmed the parts, making them insignificant. In the years since, he had not been able to grasp if that sum was the smile that made you glad, if only for a moment, that you were alive, or if it was a generosity of spirit that permitted her a fearlessness where caution would have been wisdom. Whatever it was, he thought she was beautiful.

Later, after he had given his speech about justice and equality and love and democracy and the checks had been written and he had had his hand shaken and back patted and cheek kissed and told what a good job he was doing for America, he loosened his tie and the top shirt buttons and slumped on the couch in the living room. The maid was clearing the buffet table of dishes while a Puerto Rican houseboy went through the room picking up plates, ashtrays and glasses.

"Would you like some champagne?" she asked, coming out of the kitchen with a bottle and four fluted glasses on a tray.

Her parents sat with them for a while, sipping long enough to invite him to spend the night. He stayed for a week, stayed

until her spring vacation was over and she went back to
Oberlin College. He knew it was serious because he hadn't
tried to fuck her.

He sat on the steps of the service entrance of her building.
Anyone passing by would assume he was killing time before
going inside to mop the hallways and shine the doorknobs.
He looked up each time he heard footsteps and one of those
times she came out of the building, turned south, saw him,
and hurried in the opposite direction.

He ran after her. "Amy!"

She stopped but did not turn around.

He walked up to her, his head lowered. "How are
you?"

She did not turn around but started walking. "What do
you want, Card?"

He walked beside her, not sure if he was happy that she
was as beautiful as ever. She had on a white silk blouse and
a dark jacket and pants. She was clutching a leather VIP
case in her left hand, which he was relieved to see bore no
ring. Her hair was shorter now, cut closer to the head but
still a mass of playing curls. He wondered how many cases
she had won by looking like a little girl and making an argument like a Supreme Court justice.

"What do you want?" she repeated.

He did not respond immediately, and the unusual silence
slowed her step and finally stopped her.

"I don't know," he whispered.

Her anger wanted to speak but something in Card's voice
caused her to check it.

He looked at her, and she saw the tears forming. "What
happened, Bobby?" she asked softly.

"George is dead," he blurted.

It took her a moment to find the memories to fit the name,

and when she did she found a love for Card she would have
thought had died.

"What happened?"

"He shot himself. Blew his brains out."

"Oh, God, no! Oh, God!"

1961

The first time he identified a body he stayed drunk for
three days afterward. But he was young then. Cal had asked
him to go home to Mississippi, where colored people looked
at trees and saw gallows, where when you went fishing you
thought about taking along a winding sheet because you were
as likely to reel in a dead nigger as a fish, where black babies
in the womb inhaled and exhaled fear instead of amniotic
fluid.

He was 19. If he had known how young that was, he would
not have left school. He certainly would not have gone to
Shiloh where the general store/post office on the short main
street, a white diner/bar and a colored one across the street
were the only visible sign of the community scattered along
dusty streets and roads and through the cotton fields owned
by Jeb Lincoln.

"There's a man named Charlie Montgomery in Shiloh who
has been trying to get the Negroes to register to vote."

"But what am I supposed to do when I get there?" he'd
asked Cal.

Cal smiled ruefully. "We're all new at this civil rights stuff,
Robert. You talk to people and you listen. When it comes
time to do, either they or you will know what."

Fear. One would've thought he'd get used to it eventually.
Not only had he not but the fear intensified, weaving itself
into the fabric of the ordinary and there, like larvae, ate
away the innards of dignity, feeding until neither sunlight

nor shade existed, feeding in tiny bites on the already fragile trust that he mattered in the scheme of things.

❖

the price was so high and the stakes were so low. a life for the right to cast a vote? absurd. as time went on andrea lived in a state of rage at me because i chose to risk my life and hers for some vague ideal called freedom, something i would have assumed had i been born white.

that's what it means to be white in america, even now. white people are able to make assumptions about existence that a negro can't. when you are white you assume that the cab driver who refuses to stop for you (a) didn't see you; (b) is on his way somewhere; (c) is listening to the radio and not paying attention; (d) is a son-of-a-bitch who deserves to die a slow and painful death. When you are black you are deprived of the security of such assumptions. whatever the adversity, the look of a clerk in a store to the destruction of your house by a tornado, it is safer to assume it happened because you are black. you must make that assumption because the world has never invited you to be part of it and its assumptions that constitute the norm. if you are negro, the world is to be dreaded and avoided because it is poised to kill you if you dare make the same assumptions about your existence that whites do about theirs.

murder is the act of denying another the intrinsic integrity of an existence separate from my own.

the sixties were the decade when murder became an accepted form of political discourse. kennedy's decision to send the first combat ready troops to south vietnam was an act making murder the primary instrument of foreign policy.

whom have we become that we think we have the right to decide who shall live and who shall die? perhaps it has never been any different throughout history. what is different — and this is significant — is the scale. the final solution has become a diplomatic option.

near the end andrea noticed a sadness in my eyes, a sadness that did not leave even when i laughed. she had wondered why i felt no sense of victory when i went to the white house for the signing of the 1964 civil rights act that effectively banned segregation and the 1965 voting rights act that insured the franchise for the negro. i asked her to remember, and i started to list the names of all those who had been murdered. i listed the names of those civil rights workers we knew who had spent one day too many in a mississippi, alabama, louisiana or georgia small town, who were now becoming alcoholics, who abused women, who burst into tears for no apparent reason. death had claimed their souls but, as a cruel joke, decided to leave their bodies behind.

dammit, my object had not been the passage of new legislation. i was not elated as i watched lbj sign those two pieces of legislation. i felt defeated and undone.

when i gave andrea frantz fanon's book *the wretched of the earth,* i told her, this is the future. fanon was a black psychiatrist from martinique who became involved in the algerian revolution of the fifties and treated both algerian revolutionaries and the french soldiers sent to put their fingers in the dike. fanon made a distinction between kinds of violence. i do not recall now if this was his language or if this was sixties rhetoric but the distinction was between revolutionary violence and reactionary violence. the former, he argued, was an absolute necessity, being the only means by which the colonized could liberate themselves from their state of colonization. in the blood of the colonizer, the colonized achieved catharsis. wright's *native son* had become a political ideal.

the book frightened me as nothing else had because it provided a moral foundation for murder. it gave blacks an ethical framework from which revenge became not only justifiable but necessary. the means of one's freedom became murder of the other.

even as lbj signed the bills into law, i knew we had lost.

❖

He went. The first week no one spoke to him, not even Charlie Montgomery. Why should they have? He wasn't one of them. The car in which he had driven into town could also take him away at the first sign of trouble.

Anybody could come to town and talk about freedom and registering to vote. Hell, every colored person in Mississippi knew they should be free and able to vote. That wasn't news. What they needed was to be convinced there was a way, and even if it meant wading up a bloody stream without hip boots, they needed someone to show them how to keep their balance while treading on slippery rocks. They needed someone to show them who they *could* be. They knew who they were.

Bobby's words would make little difference. Their literacy

was in the ways of people. So, he sat on their front porches and chatted about the weather and the cotton, and with the older ones he commiserated about the errancies of the younger generation, and with the impatient youth he commiserated about the blindness of the old.

Finally, one day a big man blacker than suffering, wearing coveralls and a straw cowboy hat, came up to him as he sat in The Pink Teacup, the colored cafe, and said, "I'm Charlie Montgomery." He stuck out a hand big enough to have grasped Robert's entire head, and Robert Card had found a home in Shiloh, Mississippi.

World War II had changed Charlie. "I felt like some kind of fool over there in Europe getting shot at defending a country that was killing niggers everyday. I'd lie there in them foxholes, man, the Germans zinging bullets through the air, and think to myself that if I got out of there alive, I was coming back to Shiloh and do some fighting for me and mines. You understand what I'm telling you? Me and mines!" Charlie Montgomery invited him to stay in the four-room house where he lived with his wife, Ruth.

Every morning Bobby got in his car and drove over rutted, dusty plantation roads, stopping to talk to anyone he saw about starting a sharecropper's union, or registering to vote, and almost daily there was a confrontation with some white man, a plantation overseer, the sheriff, or just a good ol' boy with a wad in his cheek and a rifle in his hand, and Bobby learned how differently the twin barrels of a shotgun felt against the stomach from the single hole of a rifle, and how different they were from the miniscule opening in a pistol, but whichever, he had to stand with the iron hole pressed into his navel and stare the white man in the eye, and the look had to be just right because if his fear showed itself as defiance, the cracker would pull the trigger, he would, and if his fear expressed itself as servility the cracker would also shoot, so the look had to be calm, relaxed, even bemused, permitting the white man the space to back down without losing face. Before the white man returned to his pickup truck, the news would be spreading throughout the Negro community. "That boy stood there and went eyeball to eyeball with that cracker as cool as morning during hog-killing time. You should've seen it!"

The colored of Shiloh had their first images of freedom.

But freedom cost, and the bill could be paid only with blood. Death had a smell to it. Bobby never knew if white people in Mississippi smelled Death, but the colored sure did.

"You be careful, son," the old folks started telling him. Maybe Negroes in Shiloh knew Death so well because it lived on the outskirts of town, sitting in a shack like an old man whose intimacy with loneliness made his only comprehensible conversations the ones he had with himself. Ol' Boy, as they called him, was moving through the world that year in a new way, not only taking people with the usual cancers, heart attacks, old age, murders, car, train, plane accidents and the freakish ones you read about in the tiny fillers in the newspaper like the girl in Germany who was playing in a cemetery and a tombstone fell on her and crushed her or the Japanese fisherman killed when a swordfish leaped from the water and with its broad bill stabbed the man in the heart and returned to the water with the grace of an Olympic diver. Death seemed to take on new life because it was the consort of the change Bobby and others his age knew had to come if they were to stand erect beneath the sky and he didn't know who Patrice Lumumba was, was not even sure how to say his name and did not know what countries bordered Zaire or where it was on the map of Africa, but he did not have to know the details to understand that Huntley and Brinkley were telling him that a Negro had been assassinated because he wanted to be free. Change was in the air like the smell of winter on Thanksgiving Day.

"Man done broke the bonds of earth," Mrs. Montgomery said with Biblical accuracy one evening sitting on the front porch looking at the paper. "Charlie, you see here that them Russians done sent a man into space and he circled the world from out where the stars twinkle?"

"Everybody wants to be free of what holds 'em down, even when it's gravity doing the holding."

It was Andrea Marshall who had shown him the paragraph in the *New York Times* about President Kennedy sending troops to Vietnam, another place Robert had never heard of and wasn't sure where it was but he understood instinctively that JFK didn't care a damn about freedom if he could send troops to Vietnam and not Mississippi. Every month he drove to Nashville for a day or two to see Cal and Andrea. Cal was still not so famous yet that he did not have time to sit around the kitchen table late at night, and the three of them would talk without purpose or direction, just talk and in the talking, learn.

"The United States broke relations with Cuba and banned travel there," Andrea said one night. "Why would this mighty nation be afraid of a small island? Why would it want to prevent us from traveling there? They must be afraid we'll learn something if we go there."

"Castro might know a thing or two about freedom that we don't," Cal commented.

Their distrust of Kennedy intensified when he founded the Peace Corps. "Why th' hell would he want to send young, idealistic Americans all over the world to help the poor when he's got Negroes in Alabama and Mississippi and Georgia and Louisiana who can use all the help anybody can give 'em?"

When Cal was angry his speech returned to the well of his southern ancestry and that was where it stayed for much of the year because 1961 was when History attached its strings to his arms and legs.

Robert knew nothing of that until he sat with the Montgomerys one evening that spring watching Huntley-Brinkley on the one channel they could get on the twelve-inch screen TV their daughter had brought them from Memphis, the only TV anybody colored had in the county, which was why the living room was always filled with people, especially at 6:30 when Chet Huntley and David Brinkley were on and it got quieter for that half-hour than it did at a funeral with no one saying a word even during the commercials as if silence were needed to absorb the pictures, not the content of the images but their mere existence as representations of the world beyond the Mississippi Delta and it did not matter if the images were of the president and his beautiful wife, Jackie, on a sailboat or of Red Square in Moscow or Alan Shephard being the first American blasted into space. What was important was *seeing* there was other than cotton and the flat delta earth and so it was that evening in May when on the TV screen appeared the image of John Calvin Marshall being dragged from a Greyhound bus by a mob of whites in Birmingham, Alabama, and beaten within a heart-skip of death, he and eleven others — colored and white — who had dared challenge the laws of segregation and sit together on a bus. They called their action "Freedom Rides," and across the South, they and anyone who worked in civil rights were thereafter known as "Freedom Riders."

Bobby had been hurt and angry Cal had not told him of the plans for the Freedom Rides, had not even hinted that such a major action was in the offing.

"Trust you?" Cal chuckled when Bobby was able to

confront him after he was released from the hospital. "If I had told you about it, there is nothing I could have said or done that would've kept you away. Am I right?"

Bobby nodded.

"What good would that have done the people in Shiloh who have come to depend on you emotionally? What would they think if you decide to jump up and go off everytime there's a bit of hot action somewhere? I sent you to Mississippi to lay the foundation for change that will continue long after you and I are gone."

The president himself pleaded with Cal not to continue the Freedom Rides into Mississippi where Cal was determined to go. Cal ignored the pleas and boarded another Greyhound bus with an integrated group and rode into Jackson, Mississippi. White Mississippi would not tolerate mob violence. The police backed a paddy wagon up to the door of the Greyhound bus. When Cal and those with him stepped off, one foot hit the pavement and the other went up and onto the steel step of the paddy wagon. Within twenty four hours they had been tried, convicted and were on their way to serving sixty days at the Mississippi State Penitentiary at Parchman, known simply as Parchman Farm.

What no one, not even Cal, could have anticipated was that the idea of the Freedom Rides caught the imagination of white college students all over the country. They began taking Greyhound buses from Chicago, Berkeley, New York, Washington, D.C., and came to Jackson, Mississippi to be arrested for trespassing, disturbing the peace and violating the laws of Mississippi, which required separation of the races except when black women held and played with and kissed and loved white babies, except when white men held and played with and kissed and fucked black women (which left black men and white women to masturbate and fantasize about each other).

By the end of the summer of 1961, several hundred young people, white and black, had been sent to Parchman, and there the civil rights movement was truly born. Sixty days in Parchman broke the spirit of petty thieves and callous murderers, but neither the warden nor the guards nor even the other prisoners understood the spirit of freedom.

"There is nothing that can be done to the man who is not afraid to go to jail or die. Nothing! The only power any government has over its citizens is the threat of imprisonment, that is, taking away one's physical freedom, and the threat of death, that is, depriving one of life. But if when you are physically free you are imprisoned in a system that tells you where you can and can't go, who you can and can't associate with, you are not free. If you are breathing but do not have the power to define your own existence, then, you are not alive. You are free when you run into the jail cell and close the door behind you. You are free when you look the marksman in the eye and say, 'Fire!' "

It was a sentiment Bobby heard Cal express first when he spoke at Fisk. It made sense until the afternoon almost a year and a half later when he was sitting in The Pink Teacup and someone rushed in and said there had been a shooting at the cotton gin and Bobby got in his car and drove with maniacal speed along the highway until he came to the un-marked turnoff by the railroad and as he slowed to a stop by the covered sheds where the wagon loads of cotton were brought to be ginned, he saw a large man in coveralls lying in the dust. Later, after Cal had served his sixty at Parchman, Bobby went to Nashville to see him and Andrea, to talk as they used to, just the three of them, but a group of brighter and more well-educated students were there now, black ones and white ones talking about this famous person who had sent a check and this writer who wanted to do an article and this TV show that wanted an interview and they looked at

Bobby as those kind had always looked at him as someone to be tolerated but only because he did the work necessary so that more important work could take place like getting Cal's picture on the cover of *Time* and having him interviewed by Mike Wallace. But Bobby insisted and pulled Cal into the kitchen and tried to tell him what it was like to see the brains of someone you loved spilling from the skull and into the dust and how you looked at the brains and wondered if that wrinkle was where sight had resided and had that crevice controlled the movement of the legs and arms and that patch of rosiness, was that where the dreams of freedom and dignity and respect came from? And he tried to describe what it was like to hold the brains of someone you loved in your hands, what it was like to try and put those brains back where they belonged except there was no skull anymore, only a fragment of bone out of which spilled brain and eyes and flies droned in anticipation of this unexpected gift of blood and how the drone and the silence were the only sounds besides the low hum of death itself and he squatted there in the dust, alone, the white men and the black who had been working at the gin standing a respectful distance away, the murderer among them, and each of them knew who he was but no one spoke and no one moved and Bobby wondered if the murderer would raise the shotgun again and shoot him but that did not happen until finally — did an hour pass? two hours? — the sheriff came and took a blanket out of the trunk of his car and covered Charlie Montgomery, and Robert, his hands heavy with the dried and caked blood, felt released and got in his car and went to tell Ruth she was a widow lady now but she knew already.

"That man would still be alive if he hadn't let me stay in his house. That man would still be alive if not for me!" Bobby finally blurted.

"He's not going to be the last one to die," Cal told him.

"You have to get used to it. The price of freedom is death."

That was not what he wanted to hear, not now, but he did not know what else to say, did not know even what he wanted to hear, and finally, he shook his head and wandered from the kitchen toward the front of the house and, surprised, found Andrea sitting quietly on the sofa, the house now empty of those intelligences feeding on themselves, and she looked up at him and after a moment, she opened her arms and he went and as she held him, he sobbed and knew that Cal was deaf to his own pain, because the cry of a people was easier to respond to than the tears from one pair of eyes, and for the first time, Bobby wondered what he was doing and why.

He stayed drunk for three days after Mr. Montgomery was killed and wanted to leave Shiloh before he got somebody else killed. The evening of the funeral Mrs. Montgomery, still dressed in black, said, "Son, you ain't goin' nowhere. We got to let the white folks know they better buy all the bullets they can find, 'cause they gon' have to use 'em on all us to stop us from getting our freedom."

He stayed and did everything he knew to force somebody to use one of those bullets — talked back to highway patrolmen, cursed the sheriff, dared plantation owners to shoot him, and he almost succeeded the night a shotgun blast covered him with glass as he lay sleeping, or the first time he took someone to the courthouse to register to vote and a mob beat him into unconsciousness.

People thought he was courageous, but courage was quiet and cautious, rooted in respect for one's mortality and the grief of those who would mourn you.

One morning at breakfast Mrs. Montgomery said, "Robert, don't you know that Charlie Montgomery will be mighty disappointed in you if you get yourself killed for nothing. Son, don't nobody blame you for what happened to Charlie.

Nobody 'cepting you. Charlie knowed what he was doing, knowed the chance he was taking. When the Lawd thinks your dying will help folks more than your living, He'll let you know."

Bobby did not feel absolved of responsibility for finding who had killed Mr. Montgomery, however. He had a feeling everybody in Shiloh knew except him, even Mrs. Montgomery, but no one would say and he could not be seen asking. So he waited until after midnight before getting in his car and driving the intricate network of the county's back roads that linked plantation to plantation. He drove slowly to minimize the noise of the car's engine and without headlights because any movement after midnight was suspicious. He stopped at shack after shack, knocked on doors until someone awoke and called out, "Who?" through the door, and hearing his name they knew his business. "Ain't nobody here seen nothing. Don't nobody here know nothing."

That's how it was for five nights but on the sixth, a door opened and there stood a small, bald-headed man as black as wet tree bark in a floor-length nightshirt . "I was dar," he said simply. "I seen. I know."

That was Ezekiel Whitson. He spoke an almost primitive English, as if he did not trust language or because he respected it so much he wanted to be careful not to abuse or misuse it. He invited Robert into the one-room cabin where he lived alone and did not light the kerosene lamp. Instead he guided Robert to a table in the middle of the room and helped him into a chair while he took the other across from him.

"Cholly would come by cotton gin a couple times a week. No reason 'cept sit and talk to us'n. Talk freedom talk. Don't care what buckra hear, don't hear. Talk freedom must act free. Cholly want us'n vote. Mistah Jeb. Cholly go to his truck to go from there. Mistah Jeb go to his truck and get he shotgun. He walk toward Cholly. When he get close all he say was 'Cholly.' Cholly turn. Mistah Jeb let go with both barrels. Cholly dead 'fo he hit the dust. Mistah Jeb put he shotgun back in he truck. Don't nobody say nothing. Buckra they stand quiet on they side of the gin shed. Niggers stand quiet on they side of the gin shed. Don't nobody know what to do 'cepting Junior who run to find you. You come. Sheriff come. We go."

Bobby left Shiloh that same night and drove to Nashville. He didn't trust calling the Justice Department from Mrs. Montgomery's phone, so he used Cal's. But the JD said they couldn't protect Ezekiel Whitson and they weren't even sure there was enough evidence to file charges against Jeb Lincoln, who would have every white man testifying that they had seen him at the opposite end of the county and what was one old colored man's word against so many whites but Bobby didn't care. "None of that matters," he said heatedly to the dispassionate voice of the Justice Department lawyer. "If you don't give Ezekiel Whitson FBI protection, he is going to be killed because he spoke with me about what he saw."

The voice at the other end of the line sighed. "I understand the pressure you people who work in those places must feel, but really, this is the United States. People don't get lynched anymore."

"You dumb muthafucka! Charlie Montgomery got lynched two months ago."

There was silence from the other end of the phone. Finally, "I'm sorry," the voice said with genuine feeling. "I'm sorry."

On Christmas Eve a loud explosion rocked the countryside around Shiloh. Robert was awake instantly, and because he slept in his clothes, he had his socks and shoes on and was out the door before the reverberations ceased echoing across the sky.

Few flames were needed to consume a tiny man in a tiny house, and when Robert arrived the fire had almost burned itself out. He could see the body as black as charred wood. This was the first bombing and Robert would learn that, depending on how close to the explosion the victim had been, generally the body remained intact, which was surprising considering the noise a bomb made.

The bomb that killed Ezekiel had been placed outside. Given the paucity of fire it had not been that well-made. Well, it had killed its target. How much better made was it supposed to have been?

In Shiloh silence was a form of communication, the heaviness of it bespeaking shame, the tension in it melting bowels into water, its heat scorching brows and burning armpits. Colored and white were imprisoned in the silence of knowledge unspoken, conspiring to keep alive a reality that would never be the same, not now, not since Death had come to live among them. No one spoke of what everyone knew. They simply waited to see who Death would take next.

Robert wanted out. Fuck civil rights! Fuck freedom! Fuck John Calvin Marshall! He was 20 years old. He was too young to be holding people's brains in his hand. He should be seeing how many pussies he could stick his dick into.

But he was supposed to have enough courage for all of them, to pry the fingers of fear from around their throats and teach them how to breathe. He could not do that if he was choking.

After a while, he could only get up in the mornings if he had spent the night at Ella's, a little juke joint on the edge of the cotton field off Highway 51. It was nothing more than a large room with a few tables, a counter, a jukebox and two pinball machines. You could get beer and if you went out back, moonshine. He always went out back. He was there every night, a bottle of moonshine in his back pocket, two dollars in nickels in his shirt pocket, and he drank and played the pinball machine. He narrowed all his attention to the metal orb beneath the glass as if by doing so, that orb would take the place of the one going in its trough around the sun. He watched the metal ball bounce off the sides and inevitably toward the flippers, which he flicked precisely to send the ball back toward the top of the machine. He didn't care how many points he made or how many games he won. He just shoved nickel after nickel in the machine until the noise of the ricocheting ball and the flashing lights, the bells and buzzers and moonshine had anesthetized him and some woman would protect him with her unadorned beauty.

But there was no protection, especially that afternoon in February of 1962 when he was driving along Highway 51, not going anywhere, just driving, not thinking about anything, especially not thinking, and when he finally noticed the flashing red light in his rearview mirror, he wondered how long it had been there and why.

"Bobby," the sheriff said simply, leaning down to stare at him.

"Sheriff Simpson," Robert said in quiet acknowledgement.

Zebadiah Simpson was not the stereotype of the southern sheriff. His stomach did not hang over his belt. Not only wasn't he fat, if anything he was underweight. He was five-six at most, and on first glance, the pleasantness of his facial expression made one wonder why he was in law enforcement. He had never been anything but polite since Bobby had come to Shiloh and even seemed sympathetic to civil rights. "I don't make the laws. I simply enforce them, the ones I like and the ones I don't."

Bobby remembered those words after Charlie Montgomery's death and wanted to ask the sheriff if he enforced the laws against murder but, hell, in Mississippi killing a nigger really didn't qualify as murder. That was more on the order of pest control or rubbish removal. You could only accuse somebody of murder if they killed a human being, and although nobody had quite figured where niggers fit, you had to be a goddam Yankee to call 'em human.

"Why don't we go over to my office in Gillam and talk, Bobby?"

Not a day would pass when he did not wish he had refused and invited Death. Sheriff Simpson was more dangerous than other sheriffs because he eschewed beatings and murders. There was a stillness in his blue eyes that hinted at an intelligence notable for a subtlety of malevolence. Where other sheriffs would have sought to destroy the bodies of those who threatened them, Zebadiah Simpson knew he needed only damage the soul. That was why he had left Charlie Montgomery to lie in the dust for two hours. That was why he never acknowledged the bombing of Ezekiel Whitson. His indifference unsettled Bobby far more than rage would have.

Gillam was the county seat ten miles south of Shiloh. Like many small southern towns it was built around a square at the center of which stood the county courthouse. In the basement of the courthouse was the jail and sheriff's office.

The office was a small room behind and to the right of the reception area. Bobby assumed the cells were behind the steel door at the end of the corridor past the sheriff's office, where he now sat staring at the large Confederate flag tacked to the wall behind the sheriff's desk.

"I want to be up front with you," the sheriff began with quiet earnestness. "If I was colored, I'd be doing what you and the others are doing. We both know that segregation is a stupid system and that it is not going to last the decade. I can hear you thinking that if that's how I feel, why don't I arrest Jeb Lincoln for shooting Charlie Montgomery and for putting that bomb outside that old nigra's shack? I reckon if I thought it would do any good, I would. But, think about it. Let's say I arrest Jeb. You don't think any jury in Mississippi would convict him, do you? So, what would I accomplish? Well, I'd probably have to move out of the state for daring to arrest a white man for killing a nigra. You understand what I'm saying."

Bobby shook his head. "Right is right and wrong is wrong, sheriff."

The sheriff smiled. "That's why I tell Jeb that you're going to win. You believe you have right on your side. You can't beat anybody who feels that way, and that's especially so if you kill them. Somebody who dies for what they believe in impresses the hell out of people. I told Jeb the worst thing he could do was kill you. Hell, if you were to get killed, you'd never die."

The sheriff got up and motioned for Bobby to follow him. He walked down the corridor, unlocked the steel door, and moved to the side for Bobby to enter first.

Bobby entered a corridor lined on each side with jail cells. The sheriff locked the door behind them and sauntered easily down the corridor.

"There were five happy men this morning when I unlocked these cells and told them they could go. I told 'em I was having a party here this afternoon." He looked over his shoulder at Bobby and smiled. "Don't you worry none. I ain't going to kill you. In fact, I'm not going to leave a mark on you. But I guarantee you when I get done, you'll never forget me."

At the end of the corridor Bobby saw two Negroes whom he recognized from Shiloh — June Boy, a big fieldhand whom he had seen at Ella's, and Wylie, who had a scar that ran from his ear halfway to his throat.

"I'm a muthafucking genius, Bobby," the sheriff said as

he nodded to the two Negroes. They took Robert by the arms and pulled him into the last cell where they threw him onto a blanket on the floor and held him down, one at his chest, the other at his legs.

The sheriff kneeled beside Bobby, undid his belt buckle and pulled his pants and underpants down to his ankles. Robert closed his eyes as he felt the sheriff's surprisingly soft hands take hold of his penis and tenderly stroke it until it, because it was it, became stiff and rigid and the sheriff reached in his pocket and taking out his pocket knife, opened it and began gently stroking the head of Robert's penis with the sharp edge of the knife blade and Robert opened his eyes and stared intently at the paint peeling from the ceiling, hoping that by doing so he could subvert his body but the excitement rose in him and despite himself, his body twitched involuntarily as the sheriff continued stroking his penis with the knife blade, lightly, barely touching the skin so that the penis hungered for the next touch as the blade went from the head down the trunk of the penis, farther and farther down until it came to the base and then slowly back up, again and again and again until the orgasm came and it was more intense than any he had ever had with a woman and his will and determination not to scream his pleasure were not enough and the release was total and complete, his aspirated screams echoing off the stone walls of the jail cell, his body arching as the semen spurted out and down his rigid penis like milky tears and Sheriff Simpson looked up at Wylie and asked, "You want to lick him clean?" and Wylie said, "Yassuh," and leaning over Robert, began licking and sucking on his penis, licking and sucking until another orgasm came, this one spreading down into Bobby's groin and thighs and up into his abdomen and chest and Robert cried because there was nothing in this godawful world like the purifying grace of an orgasm and the penis didn't give a shit about the stimulation and they left him there on the floor, limp, exhausted, sexually satisfied and intent on his own death.

That night when he went to Ella's, June Boy and Wylie were there and nobody understood why Robert, without a word, picked up a chair and hit Wylie over the head with it and when he fell, kicked him in the stomach, again and again and again, until Wylie puked everything inside him, and then did the same to June Boy. Either one could have beaten Robert with one hand tied behind his back but they did nothing to defend themselves, nothing at all and when Ella said, "Robert? What's the matter?" he screamed, "I don't know no muthafucking Robert. My name is Card. You hear me? Card, goddammit! Anybody call me Robert, I'll kill their ass. My name is Card!"

Clear-as-glass moonshine whiskey fused day into night and night into day as Card drank and fucked and slept, drank and fucked and slept, but the shame remembered him, was there waiting for him in an unexpected spasm of sobriety and lucidity until the afternoon he awoke to find himself alone.

He opened his eyes slowly. Without moving his head, he looked around. Wherever he was, he hadn't been here. He always awoke in shacks where newspaper had been tacked up as wallpaper and he could see between the floorboards to the ground beneath. There was actual wallpaper on these walls, a pattern of pink roses. Sheets covered the firm mattress, which not only was not on the floor but rested on a springbox in a bedframe with an ornate brass headboard.

"Where the fuck am I?" Card asked, sitting up. He started at the image of himself in the mirror on the dresser against the wall opposite the bed. He looked around, realizing that this was a room, not the entire house, and the door separating it from the rest of the house was closed.

He got out of the bed and peered through the window. In the distance he saw the water tower against the sky, SHILOH written large on the side facing him. There were houses around, but none he recognized. Just then he saw a plume of dust as a car went along a street. At least he was in the colored section of town since the streets were paved in the white section.

He listened but heard nothing. He found his shoes beside the bed, slipped into them and tied the laces. Quietly, he eased the door open a crack and found himself peering into the main room of the house. At the far end was the kitchen with its wood-burning cookstove. In the rest of the room there was a table around which were placed four chairs, in one corner a rocking chair, and in another, a day bed.

Card opened the door slowly and still hearing nothing, moved quietly into the main room of the house. He hadn't stayed anyplace so neatly kept since he had left Mrs. Montgomery's, not that he had formally left. He simply hadn't been back in a while, and he wasn't sure how long that was.

"Don't be scared."

He turned quickly at the sound of the voice behind him. Through the door off the kitchen from the back porch came a big man with a scar from his ear down and across his throat.

"Muthafuck you!" Card snarled.

"I ain't did nothin' to you," Wylie said plaintively. "I swear."

His voice was surprisingly high-pitched for a man so big.

"Then, what the fuck am I doing here? And where the fuck am I, anyway?"

"This was my momma's house. It's mine since she died, though I ain't never lived nowheres else. I found you laying longside the road out where that man's house was blowed up. I brung you here."

"What time last night was that?"

"It wasn't last night. It was night before."

"What? You mean I been sleep for two days?"

"I don't know as I would call it sleep. I could hear you out here twisting and turning and cussing. I thought you was fightin' Ol' Boy. I wanted to come in and see if'n there was anything I could do for you but I was afraid you'd wake up and seeing me, think something else. So, I just waited. I figured you'd have to come out sometime. If you hongry I got some string beans I canned last fall, some collards, some Crowder's peas, and I could fix up some rice to kind of hold it together."

Card hesitated, his mind wanting him to go, while one part of his body wanted to eat and another wanted to give Wylie a beating and yet another wanted Wylie to, to————

"I ain't proud about what happened," Wylie said suddenly. "I mean, don't get me wrong. I am that way, if you get my drift. That's how I got this," he added, pointing to the scar at his throat. "There was this white gentleman here in Shiloh who asked me to do that to him and I done it and he liked it. One time I guess I done it to him so good and he liked it so much that he had to cut my throat." Wylie's head was bowed, his eyes staring blankly at the linoleum-covered floor. His high-pitched voice was scarcely louder than a whisper. "If you think being a nigger is hard, it ain't half as hard as being a nigger faggot in a small town in Mississippi where everybody knows you a faggot and they treat you like shit but late at night, them's the one that come scratching at your back door. The one who cut my throat? He was the first one when I come out of the hospital in Memphis. I felt real bad about you. You can't help what your body feel. Your body don't be caring about nobody's name or whether they man or woman. It just care about itself. You couldn't help that. And you seen how that man was with that knife. If I tried to refuse, I might be wearing a scar on the other side of my throat."

Card's eyes opened wide and he started to say something but stopped. Wylie looked up at him and said, "Why don't I fire this here cookstove up and fix us'n something?"

It turned out that Wylie's mother had owned a good portion of the colored property in Shiloh, which meant that Wylie now owned it. When he offered Card a house on, ironically, Liberty Street, a block off the main street, he accepted quickly. Wylie helped him paint a sign and nail it to the roof. It read, FREEDOM HOUSE.

He supposed it was around that time he realized what he had to do and when he did, a calmness came, a peace he had never had. It would take patience and planning as well as the ability to make himself invisible. Now that he had his own house and his role, Freedom Rider, he no longer stood out. He was merely Card, who might get a little crazy sometimes, especially if he had had too much to drink, but otherwise, he was a good man. One of the best.

❖

after the lugubrious tempo of the eisenhower years no one was prepared for how rapidly history accelerated in the sixties. more happened than we knew at the time, more than we could pay attention to, more than we could know its meaning.

for example:

andrea was shaken by hemingway's suicide. i was in the midst of the freedom rides and did not know of it until she told me months later. she liked his work for reasons i never understood. i had read a novel or two and not been especially impressed. but who was i to judge? i thought spinoza was sensually exciting.

it was not that hemingway was dead. it was that he had not died. dashiell hammett, the playwright george s. kaufman, james thurber, carl jung, and gary cooper died that year. their deaths were not devastating because they were within the parameters of the normal. hemingway caused his death. he took a shotgun, opened his mouth, put the barrels inside and pulled the trigger. there was no possibility of misunderstanding his intent. ernest hemingway wanted to be dead. his death was a cultural statement, but what? perhaps it was nothing more than a reminder: in our need to bestow immortality on the living, we pressure them to remind us that they are mortal.

the measure of our lives is found in how we live with history behind the doors and walls of our homes. I do not mean history as the extraordinary events — war, depression, disaster — but those times when history does not make itself as obvious as a clown's slapstick, those times when history hums like the drone of a bagpipe, insistent, monotonous and present.

andrea and i never learned. even before i became john calvin marshall, history lay stretched in the bed between us like a child who cannot sleep. that is another difference between being white and being colored. white people can live personal lives. history does not force itself into their homes, does not sit at their dinner tables uninvited and unwanted. the negro is history, our very skin color a product of the nation's unrecognized and unacknowledged orgy of miscegenation. did andrea and i really and truly believe that we could be nothing more than dr. and mrs. philosophy professor? did we honestly think we could live personal and private lives?

when i told her that winter of sixty-one that i was going to go on the freedom rides to test the ruling on interstate bus travel, her body shuddered. she went to our bedroom and closed the door. i heard her crying but refused to go in, hold her and ask her what was wrong. why would she not cry in my presence? I would have held her then. but not when her tears were dangled like false diamonds before my eyes. if i had had a son, i would have told him that the supreme and continual test of a man is to know when a woman's tears are a plea and when a seduction.

andrea and i cared more for the images we had of each other. she had married a philosophy professor. i had married a bright and articulate young woman, well-read, someone who would be able to talk with me about anything, and we talked brilliantly as long as it was about something out there in the world. we had insight into everything except our-selves. we had compassion for everyone except each other.

for each other all we had was love, and love is not sufficient.

that is not what we are told in church, not what all the pop singers proclaim with such yearning. god is love! they shout from the pulpits. if that is so, then he is a poor lover and would be well advised to try another attribute. i think god is pain and suffering and anguish and despair and hopeless-ness because there is so much more of those in the world than love.

i learned that from lbj. he would call me late at night. it began before that awful november afternoon in dallas (an afternoon i responded to with a mixture of horror and envy because one of my responses when elizabeth passed me a note saying that kennedy had been assassinated was that his waiting was over and what a relief that must have been).

it began during the freedom rides and my frustration with the president and his brother. as i have stated, i did not like the kennedys. i never trusted them. like so many white liberals of the sixties, the president and his brother "discovered" racial injustice and were outraged. but rage is not empathy; rage is not caring. rage is even self-indulgent, a posturing that shields one from that suffering which can transform a soul.

i had been beaten severely at the bus station in birmingham. i remembered nothing, not even when i looked at the news footage, and i looked at it often because i wanted to remember the face of the man who swung the baseball bat and hit me in the head. i wanted to remember the expression on his face. i wanted to know if it had been murderous or bemused or detached. what was his relationship to his act? i never remembered.

i awoke two days later in meharry hospital in nashville, thanks to andrea who managed to send a private ambulance from nashville to birmingham to bring me back. she did not trust the white hospital personnel in birmingham. not that they would have *done* anything. i was too prominent for them to murder me outright. but medical neglect is a lethal weapon and it leaves no traces.

the human skull is amazingly hard and mine had withstood its encounter with the ash of the bat. in a few days i was at home. the beating had outraged the nation, and everyone was waiting to see if I would return to birmingham to continue the freedom rides.

robert kennedy called while i was still in the hospital in birmingham to express his sympathy and wishes for my speedy recovery and to tell me that the federal government was going to do all it could and i could help if i called for a "cooling-off" period.

i refused. the next day the president himself called. maybe it was the flat nasality of his and his brother's voices that prevented me from believing either of them. but i believed lbj.

it was the second night after i came home from the hospital. the silence in the house was thick with estrangement. andrea and i had not spoken. she was waiting to hear me say that i was not going back to birmingham. how can you speak when you know the other doesn't want to hear what you have to say?

she had gone to bed. i had fallen asleep on the couch after watching the eleven o'clock news. the phone rang.

"hello?"

"dr. marshall?"

i recognized the soft southern accent of the vice president. i had not been pleased when kennedy chose johnson as his running mate. i felt it was a sacrifice of integrity for expediency because having a southerner on the ticket might win the presidency for kennedy but it didn't bode well for the negro. i was wrong.

"i hope i'm not calling too late."

"no, sir."

"i'm not a hundred percent sure myself as to why i'm calling. i know the president and the attorney general have called and told you what they think you should do. so, i reckon it's all right if the vice president does the same thing. even if he happens to have a different opinion than the president and the attorney general. now, you might think it presumptuous for me to tell you what i would do if i were you since i'm not you, but, permit me to be presumptuous.

"quite frankly, dr. marshall, i've felt for a long time that if i was a nigra, i would kill every white person i could aim a rifle at. i don't know that the president and the attorney general understand that.

"but that's almost beside the point, isn't it? way i read it, history hasn't given you much choice. if you don't go back to birmingham and continue the freedom ride, the civil rights movement will be dead. the sale of bats will go up in the states of the old confederacy and the lives of civil rights workers won't be worth a penny. if you go back, you might be killed this time, which will be a personal tragedy only for you and your wife and your parents.

"well, i reckon that's what i wanted to say to you, though i didn't know it until i was done. forget i called. this was just one lonely man talking to another man who might be pretty lonely himself. you take care of yourself, you hear?"

the line was dead. i replaced the receiver and sat without moving for some moments, not aware at first that my face was wet with tears. there was one other, it seemed, who understood what it was to suffer history.

ANDREA

It took a while.

It took a while to put together the fragments of information that came in voices she did not recognize at first — except for Robert's. She had wondered if this was death, a shadowy awareness without the ability to communicate, self-possession without grasp of time and space. She did not know how long it had taken to understand why words loud in her mind were not so in their ears, why no one moved or responded when she reached up to touch them. A voice she knew now belonged to a black doctor had used the word, *stroke!* This was not the gentle brushing of a hand over a body but the sweep of a scythe at the base of stalks of grain, severing fruit from root.

Both her parents had died that way. "Vegetables" people had called them as they lay in hospital beds unable to move anything but their eyelashes. But when Andrea thought of a carrot, spear of asparagus, an artichoke or onion, she appreciated their colors and shapes and textures and understood their function. Should she have covered her parents with a lemon butter or hollandaise sauce, sprinkled them with salt and pepper, garnished them with a sprig of parsley? Perhaps if they had lain in bed next to a plump filet mignon she would have better appreciated them as vegetables. What purpose had they fulfilled lying in hospital beds able to move their eyes and eyelids only, one blink for yes, and two blinks for no? Yet there had been odd moments when she wondered if they had understood life and death and eternity and could not say. However, it was more likely they understood as little as she. Life, death and eternity were even more enigmatic now that she held the strands of all three.

The voices had brought her back from self-pity. Not their words, not at first, but the sounds. Robert's voice was polite, controlled, proper. There was a woman's voice, sometimes alone, sometimes with Robert, a soft voice that made her think of fudge brownies and chocolate sundaes. And there were colored voices, nurses, she understood eventually. It was their voices that had made her realize the woman was white.

It wasn't just the accent that made colored voices different. White voices seemed to come through the head. At a fund-raising party many years ago Leontyne Price had chatted about the human voice and mentioned "head tones." Andrea hadn't known that you could choose where you wanted your voice to come from — the head, the throat, the chest, the diaphragm. Thereafter she listened and heard that white people's words seemed to take a direct route from the brain to the first opening they found — the nose. Listening to them was odd because the words came from the mouth but the sound emanated in the cavities behind the nose. She found herself not knowing whether to believe the sound, the words, or neither.

The words of black people did not seek an immediate egress but went exploring through the body as if it were a vast and multiroomed cave with many corners and levels. They dipped themselves in hot springs and darkness, robed themselves in fog and mist before finally making their way along the body's narrow passageways to flow from the mouth and nose in an undulating stream whose sound had as much meaning, maybe more, than the words themselves. (That was what had made John Calvin so good. He understood the vibrations of sound that caused the soul to tremble like the skin of a drum beaten with rhythmic precision, evoking spirits from behind history's veil.)

The white woman's voice sounded as if it knew about caves, and that was surprising. Not many white people did. Andrea liked the voice, though there was a plea in it, as if it wanted something from her. When she realized whose voice it was, Andrea understood. It was not her words. Not at first. Andrea did not pay attention to them until the voice mentioned John Calvin. Except it said Cal with a tone of erotic intimacy so assumed and taken for granted the speaker was unaware of it. Such innocent sexuality was supposed to have died in the Garden of Eden.

Andrea was startled by her own lack of anger. She wanted to hear what Lisa had to say. Maybe Lisa could help her understand, though Andrea was not sure what she needed or wanted to understand. But she doubted she would have the opportunity if Lisa knew she was awake and hearing.

"Good morning."

Robert. He made it seem like all the other days. Every morning for the past — how many years? — almost twenty? he had called to see how her night had been and what her plans were for the day. He was the son she and John Calvin had not had.

She had understood that John Calvin's effort to ride history bareback made him shine like hope fulfilled. Someone had to kill him, not from racial hatred but for the erotic fulfillment. From the moment she knew, she had thought of herself as the younger woman married to a man twenty years her senior who will die before her, a woman whose years of widowhood will exceed by decades the years of marriage. The knowledge was supposed to have engendered an intense immediacy of love. Andrea imagined that was the appeal of such marriages for younger women. A couple within the same age range spent years peeing here and shitting there as they marked the boundaries of their psychic territories. With a husband whose death you could see in his eyes, there was time only for devotion or resentment.

She had thought she was marrying someone who received his doctorate in philosophy from Harvard on the day she received her bachelor's in history from Radcliffe. She had imagined a life in a small New England college town where the white spires of church steeples amid the autumn colors created a sense of eternal order and universal well-being, where she would walk quiet streets lined with maple trees and no one would have ever called her by her first name. Formality and courtesy and respect were also stone fences that made good neighbors. Intelligent, well-read, gregarious but not garrulous, friendly but not familiar, she would have done much for race relations on the campus. Her example would have encouraged the school to admit more qualified Negro students, to hire more qualified Negro faculty.

There weren't many Negro anythings at Harvard and Radcliffe when she matriculated in the autumn of 1951. She and John Calvin had not had to make an effort to meet each other because the Radcliffe dean of students and her Harvard counterpart brought them together during Andrea's first week. It could have been awkward, she supposed, but in those days white paternalism was not only not offensive, it made the difference in a world where white hostility was so much the norm that any gesture of friendliness from a white person appeared an act of senseless devotion. Neither she nor John Calvin had minded that two genteel white people who probably had never spoken to a colored person in their lives, who probably wondered what had possessed their respective admission officers to admit these colored students, nonetheless, made an effort to see that they would

not be alone. Andrea could not recall that any of her roommates or classmates ever spoke to her. Not in all the four
years did she have a conversation about homework, or snow
on the Yard, or God or sex or anything else you went to
college for. (Yet, when she became Andrea Williams Marshall, wife of civil rights leader John Calvin Marshall, it was
without shame or apology that former roommates and classmates called to tell her how much they had always admired
her and with what fondness they remembered their years at
school.)

As two Americans in a foreign country become intimates
because there is no one else to whom they can talk, so it
was with her and John Calvin. Calling him by his full given
name had started as a way of teasing him. "What a historical
burden your parents put on you," she told him. What did it
say about their marriage that she never relaxed with him
enough to call him Jack or Cal or even, honey? His seri-
ousness and intensity were as frightening as they were
compelling.

Would they have chosen each other if they had been in
their own land? If there had been other black men to choose
among, would she have found John Calvin Marshall too intense, too serious? Would he have found her — what? —
too ordinary, too prosaic?

". . . always attractive. Her hair is shorter now, but there's
still something about her. She was the first white woman I
ever spoke to. Isn't that something? I couldn't believe a white
girl that beautiful would come to a colored school in the
South. It didn't make sense. I didn't know there was such a
thing as a nice white person, especially a white woman."

It was difficult to listen when you knew you weren't supposed to. At least, to Robert. It was different when Lisa or
the doctors and nurses spoke. She might learn something
from them. Robert was more like a stuffed animal whose

presence was a vital and necessary comfort but held no answers to the riddles of your life.

Even so, Andrea did not like it when he spoke of Lisa. No woman liked to hear any man's adulation of another woman. John Calvin had never tried singing Lisa's praises to her, but he didn't have to. A woman knew a man by his touch, not his words. John Calvin's touch made her feel she was his sister. There was affection; there was caring; there was play. She would have drowned them all like a sack of kittens to have felt him desire her.

"I think I'm still awed by her, still in love with her. Not her. But still in love with what she represented in my mind when I came to Fisk. And what she meant to me was possibility. You know what I mean? If she would be my friend, someone as blond and blue-eyed and, yes, American-looking as she was, then anything was possible. It sounds silly now, and I feel foolish hearing myself say it out loud, but I don't know that we can help what we feel. You know?

"A few nights ago we went to dinner. We went to the old Union Station on Church Street. It's a fancy restaurant now, but she remembered where the colored waiting room had been. I never drive by that building without remembering but I never imagined she would remember and on her own behalf, not mine. That's what separates blacks and whites in this country. White people don't share our pain, don't want to share it, don't want to even know about it. I looked at her as she walked around what had been the main waiting room, watched her as she got her bearings, and then she looked at me, pointed, and said 'The colored waiting room was over there, wasn't it?' and I nodded and it was as if she felt the pain of all those who had sat on the hard wooden benches in that room, humiliated and demeaned. The massive granite stones of that building are awash with shame but only she and I knew. To eat there was to participate in a ritual of exorcism because every head in the place turned when I walked in with her and most of the heads stayed turned in our direction for the two and a half hours we were there."

Andrea stopped listening. After all these years she didn't want to hear, yet again, about Lisa's ability to feel the pain of black people.

She tried to stop the thoughts and feelings and was amazed that though there were few sensations in her body, words and memories still created emotion. Even more marvelous, though she hated it, was that emotions did not go away. Hurts were as knitted with color after twenty-six years of interment as they had been that day thirty years ago when he had returned from a fund-raising trip to California with Elizabeth as his newly hired private secretary.

Husbands wonder how wives know when there is another woman. It is simple. The wife feels something in her husband that has been absent. Passion. It is not just or even sexual. Passion is the love of wonder, and the wife knows when she has not authored it.

Andrea remembered looking at the two of them standing in her living room, just off the plane. There was the obvious disparity in age and the discordancy of races, and yet, they seemed oblivious of both. They were not outwardly affectionate toward each other. If they had been, Andrea thought she could have shamed John Calvin about having a "fling." Neither were they tense and ill at ease in her presence. If they had been, Andrea could have made the younger woman feel guilty for her adultery. But Andrea knew she was helpless because they shared silence so completely that it was she, Andrea, the wife, who was the guilty intruder. Was that what love was, a union not of souls but knowledge of the other exceeding knowledge of self so that knowledge of the other eventually became knowledge of self?

He had died in her arms, head against her breasts. She hated breasts and men for caring so much about their size. Modified sweat glands. That's all they were. She had looked it up once. Modified sweat glands made up of tissue and fat. What was it about large bags of flesh filled with tissue and fat and glands to produce milk? What was it that men expected of them? Were they trying to recapture an infantine innocence, preconscious memories of an Eden of soft, warm flesh against the cheeks, and milk and honey on the tongue?

She would never know. Hers had been small. She had thought they were cute, like kittens and puppies and colts were cute. He had been disappointed. She could tell because he had not touched them that first time and she had wanted him to. In the wonder of her adolescence she had wondered what it would be to have a man's hands hold one of her tiny breasts as if it were a bird, had wondered how the nipple would feel becoming erect at the touch of his fingertips, had wondered how it would be to have a man's lips and tongue and mouth at her breasts, her arms cradling him as if he were her very own child. But he had not, and eventually, she asked him, tremulously, to suck her breasts and he had and tears of gratification washed her eyes as warmth flooded her like morning over the eastern rim. But she always had to ask. He would comply but for all the pleasure it gave him, a dog would have served her just as well and, with its tongue, done better. Was there anything more lonely than knowing your husband found no pleasure from your body, not even pleasure in your pleasure?

Marriage was a succession of disappointments, the deflation of illusions until nothing remained except the person as he truly was, and that was someone you had never met. How could she have known John Calvin for four years and only discovered, within a week after they married, that he picked his nose with his finger rather than a tissue or handkerchief?

Had he not picked his nose for four years? Had he wanted to pick it for four years but held back from doing so until they were married? Or was it something the marriage brought out in him? And though she had loved his library, why had it not occurred to her that to marry him was to live with books like a sailor lived with the sea? They were everywhere, and their first fight had been over her decision to take the stacks of books out of the bathtub so she could bathe, despite his arguments for the superiority and greater efficiency of the sponge bath.

In the scheme of things, passion was without doubt the most valuable, because it was the lure that drew male and female to each other, beguiling them with fantasies of an eternity of lust and delight, and they married to ensure their eternity of sybaritism. But marriage was the discipline of learning that only change was forever, and the seeming disappearance of the qualities in the other that had elicited your passion the only constant.

Or perhaps each quality had an evil Siamese twin and she had been too young to know that John Calvin's fiery intensity was joined at the hip to an unrelenting restlessness of spirit, an inability to stop thinking and feeling and searching. His intensity had been an inspiration to Andrea the college girl. Being married to the eternal dissatisfaction of a soul seeking Truth was exhausting.

When he told her that he turned down an offer of a position at Colby College in Maine to accept one at Spelman, she cried. When she had left Charleston to come to Boston it was with the thought that she would return South only for visits. The constant assault on her dignity of segregation with its laws and signs forbidding her to do everything but breathe had taught her to hate the South with a cold and unfeeling clarity.

"A white college in Maine doesn't have to worry about

finding a good philosophy professor. White college students will learn philosophy. That's a given. It is not a given for black college students."

He was right. He always was. She did not mean that sarcastically. That was another irritant in their marriage, his uncanny instinct for the truth. He had never understood how she could remain unconvinced even when she knew he was right. Had it been stubbornness, or willful perversity? No. It had been a survival tactic, a desperate attempt to retain some scrap she knew as herself. It did not matter if she was wrong, only that she knew that she was.

She did not always know.

". . . walked around downtown. At least what was downtown back then. We stopped at what used to be Woolworth's where we were arrested that first time. We were so happy! It's amazing to think about now. We were happy to be going to jail. I don't know if I've had a feeling like that ever again in my life, a feeling of being in charge of my destiny. The outcome didn't matter. What mattered was that we were going to end segregation or die. We acted like free people."

Had that been her mistake? Had she never acted like a free woman? What if she had said, choose. Me or going South. Me or the civil rights movement. Me or Lisa. But you don't issue ultimatums if you care about the answer.

Robert wasn't free anymore. She could hear in his voice a yearning for who he had been (or who he thought he had been) thirty years ago. There had been too many days of walking through the valley of the shadow of death, too many nights of falling across a mattress with your clothes on until you couldn't sleep any other way, too many years of believing that soon peace and freedom and justice would grow like flowers in the spring and after too many times in jail and too many confrontations with highway patrolmen and county sheriffs and white men with baseball bats and shotguns and well-oiled rifles, after too many times of seeing death looking at you with a cat's indifference, one day you stopped believing and you stopped caring and when you did, you stopped knowing who you were and why. She had heard rumors that he had been committed to institutions in New York more than once. He went to Alcoholics Anonymous meetings every day. And there was something a little too ordered and too proper about him as if every ounce of energy were needed to hold himself together.

Wasn't that how she, too, had managed to accumulate all these years of twenty-four-hour days and sixty-minute hours? She had maintained control over the chaos and maybe, sometimes, it took a drink or two more than the usual to keep chaos penned, and so what if maybe, sometimes, a pill was required to put a smiley face on a hurting heart. Wasn't that better than entrusting one's soul to the chaos?

Now that the end was imminent (she hoped), she was sorry she could not put her arms around Robert and hold him like a mother and let him cry or rage, and was there much difference between the two?

How had John Calvin Marshall become the only force that had given their lives meaning and purpose, contour and texture? How had he done that, not only for them, but for an entire nation?

She didn't know. How was that possible? She had been married to the man, but if her words could have had tongue, she would have asked Lisa, who was he? That was why she had started the book. Perhaps a retrospective vigilance could redeem a slothful inattentiveness.

There could be no more lies or illusions, not with death hovering like an anxious mother at the crib of her first-born. If she didn't owe herself a certain honesty, she owed the unmitigated truth to death.

But truth could wound the heart and kill the spirit. Why?

Why did it hurt to see what was before one's eyes? That was all truth was — the acknowledgement of what is.

That was the problem. Who wanted to know what was? We wanted reality to correspond to our needs, our desires, our dreams. The only acceptable world was the one made in our own image. That was why John Calvin had been different. He saw the world for what it was and had the audacity to remake it as it should have been.

And that was why she had hated him.

And that was why she had married him.

To keep close to herself that which was most threatening, and to prevent someone else from having it close to them. She had failed. Until he was killed.

When the reporter called and told her, there was not only relief that the waiting was finally over, but an overwhelming elation that finally, at last, at last, he belonged to her. In his death, she finally became his wife and the past twenty-six years she had publicly lived the marriage that had never been.

As Mrs. John Calvin Marshall she was the guardian of his legacy and spoke on issues of national and international importance with the authority of his merit, which had automatically passed to her as his widow. When she spoke, it was as if he had not died.

No one would ever know. The last twenty-six years were also a truth, as if illusion were not a more credible and more powerful truth than bared veracity. The vice president would be at her funeral as well as leading political figures of both parties, black congressmen, entertainers and celebrities of all kinds. They would eulogize her as the widow who had been the backbone and strength of John Calvin Marshall and shouldered the burden of his vision after his death.

What harm had been done? Whom had she hurt? Hadn't she earned what had come to her? Hadn't she paid for it with loneliness as piercing as the whiteness of snow in sun-light? Hadn't she?

Yes, she had, but that could not justify self-deception, and he had tried to teach her that much. There had been no lies about Lisa. John Calvin had told Andrea about the FBI tape so that when it came she had a choice about whether to listen. She had.

Sometimes, when she focused only on John Calvin, when she thought of him instead of him in relation to her, she was surprised at an almost frivolous happiness that he had had Lisa, someone who seemed to know him instinctually, some-one with no other need than to love him. But ego cannot abide selflessness, and Andrea did not understand how the peace that came when she loved Lisa's love became a be-wildering and numbing pain when she herself posed at the center of her vision field.

Was that why Lisa had come? To help her stand to the side in her life so she could see herself? Was the pleading in her voice not a yearning for her own forgiveness but a brief for Andrea's?

But what had been her sin?

Dear God, what had been her sin?

Had it been that she had not loved John Calvin well? Had it been her unrelenting selfishness in refusing to relinquish illusion? Had it been her usurpation of John Calvin Mar-shall's legacy and subsequent presumption to immortality? Had it . . .

". . . never asked. I appreciated that. You didn't ask me any questions or anything. You took me in and found a little work for me to do around the house and let me drive you to the airport and pick you up and when I got on my feet a little more, I would go with you on your speaking trips and to meetings. You saved my life.

"I don't want you to die without knowing. Lisa gave me

the idea. She said she came because there were things she had to say even if you couldn't hear. She said she didn't know whether it was more important for her to say or you to hear and decided that all she could do was the saying. That got me to thinking about how I would feel if you died and I hadn't at least tried to tell you."

There was silence and Andrea waited, not knowing if he had paused or if time had passed and he had spoken and been gone for an hour. She heard a chair creak and then —

"George Stone. Me and him were the best two organizers in the civil rights movement. He came to Shiloh to work with me in the spring of 1963. Cal knew it was getting to be too much for me down there by myself. One morning I woke up, looked up from the mattress on the floor where I slept, and there was this nigger with a scrawny beard looking down at me, saying, 'Get up! Black folks ain't free yet!' I looked up at him and started laughing. He laughed and that was that."

There was another pause. She found herself shrinking from his voice, wanting the polite, controlled tones of the Robert she had known. This voice had serrated edges and she was not sure she wanted to hear.

"I had been thinking about it for almost a year, just waiting for the right time. I didn't know when that would be, but I knew it was going to happen. It had to happen or I didn't know if I could go on living. When George came, I knew the time was near. Near, but not yet.

"With two of us organizing, things began to happen. One of the colored preachers told us we could use his church for meetings and we started teaching people what they had to know to register to vote. Once a month the voter registration office was open and once a month, George and I would have a few people lined up at the window at nine A.M. One month the window wouldn't open until eleven-fifty-five and we would be told we were too late. The next it would be open but the clerk would spend three hours talking to somebody in the office in plain view of us in the corridor. Then, there came the month when we drove up to the courthouse and Sheriff Simpson, his deputies and damn near half the white men in the county were standing around the courthouse, lining the steps and all up and down the sidewalk. And they just happened to have their rifles and shotguns with them.

"Generally, we got to the courthouse by eight-forty-five so as to be in line when nine o'clock come around. That morning we were running late. It was me, George and two women and Mr. Peter Howard, who was almost as old as God. He had told us he would meet us there.

"I pulled the car up to the courthouse. The sheriff and his men were at the top of the steps. There must've been a hundred or so white men lounging on the lower steps and along the sidewalk. Wasn't nobody doing a thing or saying a thing. They were just standing.

"I got out of the car slowly.

" 'Where you going? What are you going to do?' George asked and started out of the car.

" 'Stay put,' I told him. 'Stay with the women.'

"I had no idea what I was doing but I knew that if we drove away from that courthouse, the movement was dead in Shiloh. My getting killed that morning would not have frightened the Negroes of Shiloh as much as my showing fear of those white men. I could feel every eye on me. I didn't wait for the crowd to let me pass but I kept walking as if expecting them to. They did, but only enough so that I wouldn't brush against anybody but still close enough to smell the Garrett's snuff, Bull Durham chewing tobacco, moonshine and sweat.

"I started up the steps, which were lined on both sides by

gun-carrying white men. I still had no idea what I was going to do or say. I figured that this was the day I was going to die and that felt good to me. Real good.

"About halfway up the steps I saw the body. It lay on its back, arms raised over its head as if they were wings in the motion of flight. He was a tiny old man, wearing the overalls of a sharecropper, overalls that had been washed so often in lye soap, they were blotchy with white spots. I saw the single bullet hole in his head, the blood congealing around it, and the flies settling on his shoulder and walking on their hair-strong legs up the neck and toward the rouge hole.

"All I could figure was that Mr. Howard had gotten there on time and started in the courthouse by himself instead of waiting for us. Obviously from all the white men at the courthouse, that day was also the day they had chosen to teach us a lesson. Mr. Howard probably saved our lives by getting killed first. Take that thought to bed with you at night.

"I willed myself not to think, not to feel. I looked at Sheriff Simpson and didn't nod or speak. I looked down at the body, at that tiny black man and felt the Mississippi heat heavy on me and heavy on him as if we were nothing more than the pants legs of a pair of trousers beneath an iron. Without a word, I stooped down and lifted the body in my arms.

" 'Card? What the hell you think you doing?'

"It was Sheriff Simpson. I lowered the body gently. 'What does it look like?' I said softly.

" 'That body has to stay put 'til the coroner comes. And he's gone fishing. I got one of my men looking for him.'

"I smiled because I was genuinely amused. 'Sheriff? You know and I know that when the coroner gets here he's going to say it was death by parties unknown. Personally, I think it'd be a shame to interrupt his fishing for something like that. I hear the catfish are biting pretty good in the Talla-hatchie this week.'

"The sheriff's face turned a dangerous red. 'You trying to be smart, nigger?'

"I didn't respond but stared at him with a look that was on the edge of defiance but didn't cross over, a look that dared the sheriff to stop me but did not challenge him, while my body stance was casual, indifferent, relaxed almost to the point of somnabulance. Sheriff Simpson didn't know what to do.

"Finally, 'Get him out of here. Dead niggers draw more flies than live ones.'

"He and his deputies laughed. I picked up the body, carried it down the steps and set it up in the backseat with the two women. Later that week at the funeral, when the preacher came to the lines in the Twenty-third Psalm and read, 'Yea though I walk through the valley of the shadow of death, I will fear no evil, for Thou art with me,' I leaped up and yelled, 'Bullshit! Wasn't nobody on them steps with Mr. Howard. Nobody 'cepting the flies. The Lord was a shepherd all right, driving his sheep to the slaughter.'

"That night George asked me what we were going to do about Mr. Howard's murder.

" 'Kill the sheriff and kill Jeb Lincoln.'

"George waited for me to laugh or crack a joke. When none came he said, 'Feels like you got personal reasons, too.'

" 'I nodded. 'Jeb Lincoln killed Charlie Montgomery and Ezekiel Whitson. The sheriff knows it and I figure he killed Peter Howard. Even if he didn't, I got my own reason for wanting to see him dead.'

" 'How do we do it?'

" 'We wait until Sheriff Simpson is out of office, which will be in November. Elections in November and he can't succeed himself. If a sheriff ends up dead, every cop in America feels threatened. Killing an ex-sheriff will not cause as much of a stir. We'll do it around Christmas when everybody is thinking about presents and getting drunk and stuffing themselves with turkey. We will fuck Christmas up for every white muthafucka in this town.'

"Then we laughed."

Silence.

Andrea remembered a night, a Christmas night. She was awakened by the sound of John Calvin on the phone, a shock and anguish in his voice unlike any she'd ever heard.

The next morning she asked John Calvin. They were sitting in the dining room drinking coffee. He didn't answer at first.

"You look worried."

He nodded. "I think I know how Jonah felt in the belly of the whale. Political movements attract the idealists and the crazed, and it is not always easy to tell them apart. But I am learning it does not matter which you are if you live, day in and day out, knowing you might die that day. I'm not talking some generalized stuff about any day might be the last day of your life. That's true but no one really believes that until it happens. I'm talking about being in your early twenties and being shot at. I'm talking about living with the knowledge that there are persons — and you know who they are — who will kill you at the first opportunity. I'm talking about going to bed at night and awakening each morning with surprised relief that you are alive.

"Andrea, what I hate this country for most is that it has forced a generation of Negro young people into an intimacy with death that they do not have the capacity to withstand."

Why had she forgotten the moments like that one, and there had been many, when they sat in the dining room drinking coffee in the morning, or late at night in the kitchen when she was getting her customary nighttime glass of milk before retiring and he would come in, not because he wanted something but because she was there and they would talk, quietly, easily, and gladness would be on both their faces. She could see the scenes in memory but they evoked no emotions. Why did she remember the pain more easily? Even at the core of their moments of intimacy, had there been a hollow place where the heart should have been?

She envied Lisa the love that remembering released for her. How incredible it must be to remember and to reenter the love, even though the other is no longer present. It did not matter. Relationship did not require fleshly immediacy. Only submission.

"I never told anyone why I cracked. Not Cal. Not even the psychiatrists. George was the only one who ever knew.

"On Christmas Eve the sheriff and Jeb Lincoln would have a little party at the jail for anyone that wanted to drop by. They'd drink a little moonshine and everybody would get a nice buzz on. Nothing heavy because they had to look halfway straight to go to church the next morning and for dinner at their momma's houses. The sheriff and Jeb Lincoln lived on adjoining pieces of property and I guessed they would drive home together in Jeb Lincoln's car. They lived on a dirt road off the main highway. About a half mile after you turned onto the road, it went down a little hill. At the bottom of that hill was a huge oak tree that sat back. It was the perfect place for an ambush. We could park the car in the shadows of the tree and no one would ever see us. When we heard them coming, I was to pull our car out into the road and block it. Before the sheriff and Jeb Lincoln knew what was happening we would jump out of our car, shoot them, get back in our car and be on our way.

"Well, 'long about ten-thirty we heard the car coming. You live in a small town you learn to identify people by the sound of their cars. That's true! Mr. Montgomery taught me that. Wasn't a car in the county sounded like Jeb Lincoln's. It was a Buick and he kept that baby in mint condition. It was the one car that you almost couldn't hear.

" 'They're coming,' George said.

" 'I hear 'em,' I answered. I was supposed to turn the key and start the engine. My fingers were on the key, but I didn't turn it.

"The car was closer.

" 'Start the engine!'

"I couldn't turn the key. I could feel the lights of Jeb Lincoln's car coming down the hill. George reached over and tried to turn the key. I grabbed his wrist. I'm still not sure why.

" 'Goddammit, nigger! Start the fucking engine. Turn the goddam key!'

"I held his wrist so tight I was afraid I was going to cut off the circulation to his hand.

" 'Fuck you, muthafucka! Fuck you!'

"The car drove slowly past us. I watched the red eyes of its taillights recede into the distance. When I couldn't see them anymore, I turned the key. The engine started. Slowly I turned the wheel and made a U-turn and headed for the main highway. I didn't know I was crying until George asked me if I was OK. Then I became aware of the wetness on my face. I heard a low-pitched moaning and knew it was me.

" 'You OK?' I could hear concern in his voice. 'I'm sorry I said what I said to you. Hell, them crackers ain't worth killing.'

" 'But they are,' I said, my voice cracking with tears. 'They are! I froze, man. I froze! I was scared to kill a white man. I was scared, man!'

" 'Don't worry about it, homes.'

"We were at the main highway now. I turned left and

headed back toward town. 'Tell me the truth. You weren't scared, were you?'

"There was a long silence. Finally George said, 'I ain't been through what you been through down here. Maybe I didn't know enough to be scared.'

"I knew otherwise. I had failed. How the hell could I be free until I could do to a white man what white men had no problem doing to us? How could Negroes be free until we made white people as afraid of us as we were of them?"

Andrea stopped listening. Here, waiting patiently and eagerly in Death's vestibule she understood — too late — that until we knew the pain of another, our relationships were no more than exercises in an acting class. Until we knew the sizes and shapes of our own pains, and more, allowed someone else to glide their fingers over their misshapen contours, we were no more than shadows on the wall of a cave. But there was something more, it occurred to her as Robert's voice was breaking through again. You had to love the pain with all the fervor of teenage lust. And when you did that, you ceased judging others; morality was no longer a simplistic good against a one-dimensional evil. Instead it became labyrinthine and twisted and turned back on itself and good changed into evil and back again until each ceased being distinct and separate and became instead a new kind of whole constantly shifting and rearranging its parts. To be moral was to live one's singular and unique truth, regardless of the price, and there was always a price, she suspected.

"I had dropped out of Fisk at the end of my freshman year to follow Cal. I was 18 years old. Eighteen! Can you believe that? Eighteen years old and I go to Shiloh, Mississippi by myself to face down death. I am 19 when I sit there in the dust trying to put Mr. Montgomery's brains back in his head and six months later, Ezekiel Whitson is murdered.

"I was too young, Cal. You took my love for you, my eagerness, my naivete, my idealism. You took everything about me that I loved and I'm sorry, Cal, but youth and love and eagerness and idealism are no match for evil and hatred and violence. Yes, we won. Would you believe that the sheriff in Shiloh is a black man now? But, dammit, I think Mr. Montgomery and Mr. Whitson and Mr. Howard and me and George were too high a price."

He was crying, and grief swelled in her, unwelcome and unwanted. Grief was not deterred, however. It had waited so long for her to acknowledge its being. It would wait beyond death if it needed to.

"George," his voice said dully after the choked sobbing ended and silence calmed them both. "That's who I wanted to tell you about. Don't ask me why. It's like Lisa says: you do what you feel like you need to do; you do what you think is right. Maybe you understand why. Maybe you don't.

"I couldn't stay any longer. That same night I called Cal and he knew I had lost it. He sent Lisa down that night and she drove me from Shiloh straight to a psychiatric hospital in New York. George stayed. He married a local girl. Mamie. Her skin was so black it shone as if it had been polished. She was extraordinarily beautiful. I ended up living with a white girl. Amy. She was beautiful, too. She loved me, which wasn't easy to do. I have only vague memories of many of those years. If I wasn't drunk, I was on pills to control my depressions or on pills to control my highs, and when the alcohol and the marijuana and the pills wouldn't work, I was in the hospital strapped to a bed.

"During the few times of something resembling lucidity I would leave and come here to Nashville and somewhere in there Kathy and I got together and suddenly, I had a child. Kathy wanted me to be a husband and a father. I could have more easily become white.

"It was 1973. Clarity. When you can remember the year something happened, you are paying attention to your life. 1973. I was living with Amy again. It was the best time we had together. I wasn't drinking nonstop. Nothing helps a relationship more than being conscious of what you're doing and saying.

"It was spring. George showed up one afternoon at our apartment. Whenever he was in New York raising money for the farmer's cooperative he had organized, he stayed with us. In New York it was easier for him and me to be together. He still respected my organizing skills and we would talk over problems he might be having in the community. He always made me feel good by telling me that people still remembered when I did this, that or the other. He always seemed to arrive an hour or two before Amy was due home from work, and sometimes he would cook and sometimes she would and we would spend the evening laughing and talking and sharing that incredible intimacy that comes when people know the worst about each other and love survives.

"This day, however, George called first and wanted to know if Amy was there. When I told him she was at work, he asked if he could come over. When he walked in, he was quieter than usual and his quietness was tight. I wondered who had died or been killed in Shiloh.

"We sat down at the round oak table in the dining area off the kitchen. I poured him a cup of coffee from the always plugged in percolator. We chit-chatted aimlessly for a few minutes and I waited.

"Finally, without prelude, he said, 'I can't keep quiet about it any longer, Card. It ain't right. It just ain't right you being with a white woman. It ain't right.'

"But before I could say anything, and I was too stunned to know what to say, he continued. 'But I guess you say that's my problem.'

" 'You're right,' I said flatly.

"There was a long heavy silence. Finally, he stood up. 'Got to be moving on down the road. You take care of yourself, Bobby.'

" 'Yeah, you, too.' I don't know if he was waiting for me to offer my hand, or if I was waiting for him to offer his, but we stood there facing each other for a long moment, not moving, not speaking, just waiting. But there was nothing to say. There was nothing to do. He turned and went toward the door. I followed, held it open and closed it softly behind him.

"That was the last time we saw each other. I was hurt and angry that he had sat there so many times, had eaten Amy's cooking, had hugged her like an old friend, had laughed and joked with us. I thought he was a total hypocrite. Five years later, after he was dead, I had a new thought. All the time George had spent with me and Amy hadn't been a lie. It had been love. He had tried to accept what for him was unacceptable. He had tried and it was not that he failed but there came a moment when he did not have the energy or simply could not continue. I, in my self-centeredness, had perceived what I deemed his failure and ignored all the times he had succeeded.

"Kathy called me when he died. Suicide. I couldn't believe it. George? Kill himself? I didn't know what to do. Even though I hadn't seen or heard from him since that last time at the apartment, I suppose I had counted on him being in the world, being down there in Shiloh carrying on our work.

"I went to the funeral. It had been fourteen years since I had left Shiloh. The funeral was long and sad as black funerals can be, especially in the South. And someone like George had to have a good send-off and they gave him that. That church rocked with music and words.

"Late that night, after Mamie was asleep, I went by The Pink Teacup. It hadn't changed one bit. Even the flies were the same ones. After everyone had welcomed me back and we had reminisced about the old days, which were a helluva lot sweeter in retrospect, I settled down at my customary table in the corner. Somebody got me a bottle of white lightning but I stayed with the ginger ale I was drinking.

"Wiley came over and sat down. He had been elected county tax assessor. I don't need to tell you that the last thing you do is rush a southern Negro to tell you anything, even the time of day. We must have talked about an hour. I suppose it took Wiley that long to ascertain whether I would want to hear what he had to say, who I was now as opposed to who I was then.

"Finally, 'It was too bad about George.'

"Wiley wasn't extending idle sympathy.

" 'What happened?' I wanted to know.

" 'You know that road what goes out to Jeb Lincoln's place.'

"I couldn't speak. I just nodded.

" 'And you remember how the road goes down a little hill and at the bottom of it, there's a big ol' oak tree?'

"I nodded again.

" 'Well, that's where they found him. He was sitting in his car parked off the road underneath that tree. A bullet was in his head and the gun was in his hand. Why do you think he went out there to kill himself?'

"I shook my head again. I had hoped for some answers from Wylie, and it seemed he was hoping for the same from me. What had happened? George was accepted in the community. The farmer's co-op had white as well as black farmers in it. It didn't make sense.

"I've read a lot of books on suicide since then because I still don't understand. From what I can gather it seems that suicide is the ultimate act of anger. So I tried to think what George was angry about. Was he angry that we hadn't killed Sheriff Simpson and Jeb Lincoln? It took me a while before I realized that I was asking the wrong question. It wasn't what he was angry about. It was who he was angry at. And there was only one person who understood the significance of the place.

"The next morning I got in my rental car and drove back to the airport in Memphis where I turned the car in. I got on a plane and came here to Nashville and around one o'clock that afternoon I rang your doorbell. The rest, as they say, is history."

And if she could have spoken, what would she have said? Because she did not know, she was glad she could not speak, glad he did not know that she had heard. However, she suspected his life would resume now. He had heard aloud the worst he could say of himself, and he had survived.

Suddenly, she was afraid. Was she to die and never have uttered a word of truth? But how could one deprived of speech speak the truths that desperately needed saying? She doubted that she even knew her truths, and now, before it was too late, she so desperately wanted to. But how? How? And the answer came even as the question continued to unfold.

❖

both lbj and i have been abused by history. we knew we would be. but he knew it almost immediately after he took the oath of office on air force one in dallas on that fateful november day.

frankly, once he was thrust into the presidency, i did not expect to hear from him anymore during the troubled hours of the night. so i was surprised when the phone rang the night of kennedy's funeral.

"cal," the voice said flatly.

"mr. president," i responded.

"shit! i didn't call you in the middle of the goddam night to be reminded of what i don't want to be reminded of. dammit, cal!"

"better safe than sorry."

"you right about that. sitting in the oval office can give a man some dangerous ideas about who he is."

i detected a weariness in his voice different from the exasperated weariness of being ignored as vice president.

"you sound tired," i told him.

"worse. scared."

"of assassination?" was the logical question.

"naw. history has dealt me an unplayable hand. no vice president who has come into office after the assassination of the president has ever succeeded. And if that vice president is tall and ugly and has a southern accent, and if that president was young and handsome with hair that blew in the wind, that vice president will never be loved by the people. he'll be damned lucky if they like him, especially after he replaces the president's brother as attorney general."

"you're going to do that?"

"generally i would rather have my enemy pissing on the inside. i prefer this one on the outside. there's a better chance the wind will blow the piss back in his face. however, it's a no win situation. if i keep him at justice, he'll use it as a powerbase around which the kennedy crowd can gather and try to undermine me from within. if i kick his ass out, he'll try to undermine me by running for the presidency, which he is going to do whether he is in or out of government. jfk's assassination has elevated the kennedy name to the equivalent of a moral crusade for decades to come. now, you tell me. what chance does a po' white cracker from texas have against that?"

"not much," i had to acknowledge.

"and what pisses me off is that i am going to get a better and stronger civil rights bill through congress than him and his brother could have ever gotten through, but guess who'll get all the credit? i'll be seen as carrying out kennedy's program. shit!

"the civil rights bill he was proposing was a crock. i knew it. you knew it! hell, if jack and bobby cared as much about civil rights as they did pussy, every negro would have forty acres and two cadillacs in the garage. i've been in politics all my life and i know politicians like to fuck more than most, but i ain't never seen two boys hunt poontang like them two kennedy brothers.

"shit! imagine their surprise when edgar pulled out pictures from his private collection. i've got to move bobby out of justice. you can't have the director of the fbi in a position where he can wield power over the attorney general because he has pictures of the sumabitch with a mouthful of pussy. incidentally, edgar was over here today after the funeral. i figured he'd show up the first chance. he come showing me some pictures of you among a lot of others. even had a few of me in compromising positions. i've known edgar since 1945 when i bought a house on the same street he lived on. hell, he was like an uncle to luci and linda and me and him had long chats on many a sunday afternoon. between the two of us there probably isn't anybody who matters that we don't know something dirty about. even though me and edgar have been friends for a couple of decades, i wasn't naive enough to think that he didn't have a file on me. hell, friendship is one thing, but power is damn near as good as sex. but you got to watch out for somebody who thinks it's better. like that nixon. anyway, i didn't blink an eye when edgar showed me my file. he expected me to be indignant or embarrassed. to tell the truth, i was disappointed. the photographs were so grainy and out of focus i wasn't sure it was me, and damned if i could remember who the woman was until i looked through the reports and found her name. got me to wondering what had happened to her and where she was. she had been a good piece. well, anyway, i closed the folder and i know edgar expected me to pass it back to him. i put it in the top drawer of my desk and looked at him benignly. he wanted to say something, but what the hell could he say? i was the president of the muthafucking united states. i'd been waiting for this moment for a long time. i reached in my file cabinet — we met at my office in the executive office building. i don't want to move into the white house too soon and make it seem like i'm anxious to get mrs. kennedy out. anyway, i reached in my file cabinet and came out with a folder of my own. i threw it on the desk. he opened it slowly and almost shit his pants. i got pictures of him in women's clothes running around at a faggot party in new york. shit, if jack and bobby had treated me with a little respect i could have gotten edgar off their asses. but fuck 'em. anyway, you don't have to worry about edgar. in fact, i told him to keep me updated on all the new pictures he got of anybody so i could add them to *my* collection, which is almost as good as his."

i never told anyone the details of those late night phone calls. only andrea knew of their existence even. i don't know if it is true of everyone but certainly those of us whose private lives have been swallowed by the public personae need one relationship so unusual and so secret that no one would ever suspect it existed.

lbj and i genuinely liked each other. we shared that peculiar bond black and white southerners have. northerners do not understand that blacks are as much southerners as are whites. the master and slave historical relationship may appear from the outside to have been one of oppressor and oppressed. from a political perspective that is so. however, lbj and i both were aware that black and white southerners shared and suffered slavery together and that we as its legatees carried the burden of that history. lbj remembered what he had not suffered in the flesh. That is the key if a white man is to relate to a black. to remember another's story as your own. jfk and bobby never knew there was a story and i think they hated lyndon so fiercely because he did.

lyndon's tragedy was that he didn't understand which story was truly his. he was the wounded healer who tried to live the warrior's story. he tried to use the sword to arbitrate good and evil. jfk could have. lyndon could not.

one of the cruelties is that all too often we are remembered either for what we did poorly or for what we did not do at all. lyndon is remembered for vietnam. he is not remembered as the president who put a finish to the legal structure that had been segregation and disenfranchisement. but, if truth be known, he is scarcely remembered at all.

at least there is a day named for me.

better to be forgotten.

no, history has not been kind to either of us. lyndon knew when he took the oath of office, jackie kennedy present in her blood-stained suit. i knew when a young heavyweight champion named cassius marcellus clay announced that he was, in reality, a member of the nation of islam and was henceforth to be called muhammad ali.

what did i know? that the subterranean stream of racial chauvinism, which had coursed beneath the strata of black existence for a century, had broken through to the surface. and once there, it would drown us all.

LISA

Thursday, 10 P.M.

It says a lot about our marriage that I sit here in a Holiday Inn and choose to communicate with you on my laptop. And who knows? I may even upload this when I'm done and e-mail it to you. Then again, you may never read it. But it is a sign of something, I suppose, that I want to speak to you, but talking to you on the phone would be too immediate. I can scarcely possess my thoughts and find words to express a fraction of them before being distracted by the jab of one of your "What do you mean?"s or a silence so heavy on my ears I feel I am being pulled to the ocean floor, and when you get silent like that I can become so entangled in what I *think* you're thinking that my thoughts turn to sand, run through my fingers and cover the tops of my shoes.

But electronic mail has all the immediacy of a phone call without the distraction of your emotions, the intimacy of a letter without the hole in time between expression and reception. If e-mail had existed when we met, we could've had a wonderful relationship and never needed to marry, or even meet.

So, where have I been for the past ten days, you want to know? I am at a Holiday Inn in Nashville, Tennessee, sitting at one of those round hotel tables over which hangs a lamp with a two-watt bulb in it. The table is in front of a pair of hotel windows that look like sliding doors until you try to open them. It is impossible to be in a hotel room and have fresh air. Then again, these days the freshest air probably comes through the ducts in hotel rooms.

The genius of the American hotel room is that it does not ask me to adjust to its personality or history because it has neither. It is a psychically neutral space into which you can bring whomever you are and know it will be received. (That's more than a lot of us can say about home.)

Across the street, West End Avenue, is Centennial Park. At the far end of the park is a full-scale replica of the Parthenon. I lived here for almost seven years and never got used to driving by and seeing one of the most famous pagan structures in the Western world.

I've never been in the park. Blacks were not allowed thirty years ago. My credibility and trustworthiness depended on not taking advantage of my whiteness and eschewing the social privileges white skin gave me. Oh, there were times I wanted to sneak off for a steak at an exclusive restaurant or check into a hotel and spend the weekend having room service and taking bubble baths. But I didn't. And I never went walking through Centennial Park or sat on the steps of the Parthenon. I won't even now. Those of us who remember "then" have an obligation to it. It isn't right that white people in the South walk around as if segregation never happened. How dare they act as if they don't need to remember what southern blacks cannot forget. That is the sin — to live as if you have no responsibility for the pain of others.

Bobby and I were talking the other night about how angry we are. Bobby is Robert Card. He was a freshman when I was at Fisk and had a crush on me, he maintains. I didn't know. He dropped out of Fisk to work for Cal in Mississippi.

I never knew what happened, but Cal sent him to New York to fund-raise, which he did well for a while. He told me what the years have been like for him, years of drinking, of fights, of months in hospitals, sometimes in strait jackets, always on tranquilizers of some kind.

He has been OK now for almost for fifteen years, though he still takes medications and goes to AA meetings every day. Sometimes, a lot of times, he can't sleep until he gets up, dresses and lays across the bed atop the covers. That's how he slept when he was organizing in Mississippi. He says he knows no one is going to drive by and shoot in his house or throw dynamite on the porch, and he shrugs with an embarrassed helplessness and bewilderment.

I understand the power of memory to seize the soul and hold it close, stopping time. When time stops, life stops. Oh, gray comes into the hair, and the hips widen and the breasts sag, but this deterioration of the flesh is programmed like baby teeth.

I understand because I look back and see nothing I can call a life. Bobby has a child, at least. Adisa. She is 22 and lives here. Last week he invited me to dinner at his house — me, Adisa and her mother, Kathy. I think he wanted me to be a witness that he had accomplished something in his life.

His daughter is in law school at Vanderbilt. When she told me I started to say that Vanderbilt didn't admit colored but that was thirty-two years ago in a Nashville, Tennessee, that exists only for the emotionally disabled like me and Bobby. I do not know the Nashville, Tennessee, in which Adisa grew up, a Nashville where black and white went to movie theaters together, sat at lunch counters, ate rare steaks in the same restaurants, those who could afford steaks. I cannot imagine a Nashville, Tennessee, in which one does not need to be afraid.

I did not remember Kathy though I pretended I did. She is small, with dark skin, and a graying Afro shaping her tiny face. She works for a social service agency of some kind. She and Bobby never married and do not live together now. She still loves him. I could tell by the avidity of her gaze as he set food on the table.

Bobby does not see her love. He cannot receive what he does not know exists. She knows and it hurts. He is still in love with Amy, a white girl he lived with in New York back in the seventies, but he doesn't know if she is dead or alive or even where she is.

The three of us sat at the dinner table attentive to her or his private sorrow and Adisa sat among us, oblivious to how much pain a person can have and still live. She will learn because the extent of one's maturity depends on how you live with your pain.

I admire Bobby because after all these years, he is still trying to get it right. He is still trying to figure out what you have to do in this life to be able to lie down at night with a measure of peace.

I certainly don't know.

"I was always curious how you got to be Cal's girl Friday," Kathy asked pointedly but without hostility when we were having dessert.

I shrugged. "Whenever he needed something mundane done, I would do it. And nobody else wanted to do things like make plane reservations, keep his appointment calendar, remind him when he had to do this or that, not to mention be on call twenty-four hours a day and be prepared to go anywhere at anytime."

Kathy smiled finally. "It's good to see you, Lisa. And it's good to see you haven't changed."

"What do you mean?"

"We, meaning the black women, always respected you. You didn't play power games; you didn't try to lord it over us because you were the only one who had instant access to Cal. At the same time, if we needed to ask him a question or get a message to him, you wouldn't act as intermediary but make it possible for us to see Cal ourselves. At the same time, you acted as Cal's eyes and ears and if we wanted Cal to know something, we only had to mention it casually to you. You kept your counsel. And, from the way you just answered me, you're still doing the same."

I looked at her and could not tell if the last comment was honed. She was smiling, but I had always marveled at how black women could smile an anger. I could feel a tight stillness at the table and I desperately wished I could think of something witty to say that would enable us all to breathe again. But I'm not even one of those who thinks hours later of what I should've said.

"Perhaps that is why Cal trusted you so much," she said suddenly. "Perhaps that is why we did, too."

"Thank you," I managed to respond.

We all breathed again, but I still did not know whether to believe her. And, I found that I did not care. I have little patience with the resentment of black women toward white women, with their accusations against white women for taking "their men." Black women have written about how disgraceful and embarrassing it was that John Calvin Marshall died in the arms of a white woman, and what was he doing coming out of a motel with a white woman anyway?

It appears that many blacks (and forget whites) cannot grasp the simple fact that love is private and no one has the right to judge anyone for whom he or she loves or how.

When I left I wondered if Kathy loves Bobby or does she merely want him to stop loving Amy?

Friday, 1 A.M.

I have been away ten days and I see on the Weather Channel that it has snowed twice since I left. How dare nature produce snow without me there to appreciate it? Here, it is already spring. I had forgotten how early and quickly it comes in the South. In Vermont the light is still thin and will remain so for another two months. Here the light is robust, a bright shining portending the heat of summer.

Nashville has changed but only superficially. It has expressways now, which any municipality must have if it is going to puff out its civic pride and call itself a city. The expressways have huge signs hanging over them directing you to Knoxville and Memphis and Louisville, as if there is no reason to exit in Nashville. The local exit signs are few and aren't very helpful if you don't already know how to get where you want to go, and if you already know, you don't need them.

Nashville is a small town pretending to be a city. It has a couple of tall buildings, the state capitol, the Country Music Hall of Fame, Grand Old Opry and a number of colleges and universities — Vanderbilt and Fisk being the most well known. But everyone drives slowly, except on Friday and Saturday nights, and people speak to you in stores and on the street as if you'd been at their house yesterday for coffee, and you regret that you hadn't.

When I drove in from the airport I was lost until I saw an exit sign for Jefferson Avenue. Jefferson goes by Fisk. Fisk is in the opposite part of town from the Holiday Inn but I knew the preexpressway route to it from there.

I stopped by the school before going to the motel. As I went onto the campus, emotions came with the rush of bats from a cave at dusk. I had no idea why or from whence came this pain and the sob I refused to release. There were emotions in my heart and images in my mind, but the emotions were not evoked by the images. I felt like a Picasso with an eye in my skull and a tear at my navel.

The images in my mind were like the ones we see of our parents when they were young, photographs taken before we were born or even thought of (and don't you resent that your parents had lives and were even happy before you came into existence?). Although there is a resemblance between the people in the photos and our flesh-and-blood parents, we don't know the people in the photographs. We do not want to share in those smiles that were smiled before we were born. Those people have no presence in our souls, and neither do our parents as long as the two in those old photographs remain images. We want to confine the lives of our parents to the parameters of our relationship to them, which means we have no interest in them as they are. But if we are somewhat awake in our lives, we will recognize that such an attitude brings us mouth-to-mouth with our own self-centeredness. If we can withstand the self-disgust, we have stumbled onto the narrow trail to wisdom.

These images were of me, however. I went into the chapel, a round building except at the far end where the choir loft and pulpit are, went up to the balcony and sat where I had the day I first saw John Calvin Marshall. No emotion. I came down and stood in the foyer where we met and recalled him addressing me as Elizabeth, a name no one before or since has called me by. No emotion.

However, as I came out of the chapel I happened to look west across the campus and saw a tiny red-brick building. Feeling and memory joined.

When the photographer and art patron Alfred Stieglitz died, his widow, the painter Georgia O'Keefe, wanted to give his art collection to those who did not have ready access to art. So, she divided his collection into three parts and gave one-third to a small black school in Nashville, Tennessee, Fisk University. Though O'Keefe did not have someone like me in mind as being among the art-denied, I loved that gallery and that collection.

It was there I learned about early twentieth-century contemporary American art — Arthur Dove, Marsden Hartley, O'Keefe, of course, John Marin — how I loved his watercolors and the way he broke light into splinters to achieve luminosity. I also saw the work of black artists for the first time and remember in particular a Romare Bearden rendering of the crucifixion.

I went by the gallery but it was closed. So I sat on the steps and, suddenly, all the joy and lightness and wonder that is yours simply because you're 19 and have no doubt that you are immortal returned and I was again that girl who had sat on the benches of the gallery staring at the captured images of color and line, not knowing what I was seeing as much as I was enthralled and exhilarated that I could see. I suppose that is the function of visual art — to make you glad that you can see. And I remembered the woman of the later years who came home to Nashville tired after a week, a month, three months on the road with Cal, and often I would find an afternoon to go to the gallery. Those paintings became a still point that held me fast in time and space, and I could remember there was a realm where race did not matter, where people did not express how much they despised themselves for being white by proclaiming their whiteness superior. As I sat on the step in the surprise of gladness at whom I had been, I was happy that Georgia O'Keefe had given the paintings to Fisk and the sob broke open and I cried because I had never written to tell her what a difference her gift had made in my life, how it had sustained me and now she was dead and I had not said thank you.

When the tears stopped and I was walking back to my

rent-a-car, a Blazer, of course, I realized that during those moments on the steps, memory and emotion had been one and I had dwelled in my life with all the ease of a tent dweller in the desert.

That's how it is when I ski or hike or even now, sitting here before the computer. I love the computer, Gregory. I even love DOS! Skiing and hiking and computers. What's the common denominator? All three bring me into magic, into a realm of enchantment. Anything that places us in the presence of or gives us access to the power of dismay enables us to be in a relationship with magic.

I don't know what that means, Gregory. But I don't have to understand something to know it's true.

The older I get the less I understand about who anybody is and why we do what we do. Why are you a dentist? Do you like teeth? But how can anyone *like* teeth? How does one *choose* to spend his life sticking his fingers inside people's mouths? We've been married twenty years and I haven't figured it out, Gregory. Did you just wake up one morning and say, 'Damn! What a way to spend a life!' I thought I would, in time, get used to being touched by hands that groped in people's mouths, hands bathed in the spit of a humanity that can't find a cure for halitosis. I never have. The thought of your spit-covered hands touching me has made me nauseous for twenty years and I'm sickened I feel like that.

I got into a conversation once with a gynecologist's wife. I think it was at some dental convention back when I was still trying to figure out what a wife was and what the hell she did. (Gave up on that pretty quickly, didn't I?) There was also a convention of gynecologists going on at the hotel and we happened to meet in the hotel bar. I asked her if she responded sexually when her husband stuck a finger in her vagina or anus while they were making love, or did she wonder if he was giving her an exam, or did she ever wonder if he could tell if she were having an affair by feeling inside her vagina? Did she ever wonder why a man would want to spend his life sticking his finger in vaginas and was he getting a secret sexual thrill from doing so? And did thinking about all these things, if she did, make her frigid? She slapped my face, or would have if my athlete's reflexes hadn't made me grab her wrist. I'm not sure we are supposed to understand our lives, Gregory. Isn't it enough to live them with whatever spirit we can muster?

You know by now that Andrea Williams Marshall died today. I watched the reports on TV tonight. She was an impressive figure when the cameras were rolling. At a time when so much of public discourse consists of the projection of an image that will evoke warm feelings rather than thought, Andrea Marshall had her place. By her adopting the role of the widow, the nation was forced to remember John Calvin Marshall, and remembering him, it could not totally lose touch with some vague notion of racial equality and justice.

I came here to be with her. When I left ten days ago, all I knew was that I had to come. Once here and once it became clear that she was not going to recover, I knew I had come to hold her as she died, to hold her as I had held Cal, and I was with her when she died.

Daddy had a heart attack and was dead within hours. He never regained consciousness and if he had, I could never have gotten there in time. Jessica developed Alzheimer's. God, I hated her for doing that. I know that sounds stupid, but you didn't know her. I have no doubt she developed Alzheimer's so she wouldn't have to try and communicate with me, so she wouldn't have to take responsibility for what and who she had been. She always thought I wanted her to apologize for the love she failed to give me. I wanted far more than an "I'm sorry." I wanted her to take responsibility for failing me. She made sure she wouldn't be able to do that. Sixty years old and she didn't know who I was, who she was or where she was. I would sit by her bed in the nursing home wishing I could understand why she had been in the world. What difference had it made that she had lived? No one had loved her. Not daddy, not me. She died suddenly in the middle of the night, as you probably remember. When they called and told me, I wanted to tell them to put her body in a Glad trash bag and put it out on the curb.

Once you reach a certain age, each death demands a re-living of the previous deaths in your life. I pity you that your parents are still living. No wonder you can't grow up. As long as you are a son or daughter, you cannot occupy your own place in the world. The deaths of our parents is the fortuitous loss that forces us to fill this raw and new emptiness with ourselves — whoever that is.

I know one of the reasons you wanted to marry me was because I had been a part of history. You were proud to have as your wife the woman who had been John Calvin Marshall's personal secretary. I was amused and I shouldn't have been. If I had known better, I would have been outraged that you dared put your fantasies on my life. But I was amused. Maybe I was even flattered. I was important in your eyes. I had been an intimate part of the life of one of the great men of the twentieth century. I'm not sure anymore how true that is. I'm not sure if it was ever true. I wonder if I have not been a fantasy in my own life.

You probably think Andrea and I were close because I came to be with her as she lay dying. We were not. During the years I worked for Cal, I don't know that all the sentences Andrea and I exchanged would make a page of double-spaced text. There were weeks when I was in and out of her house daily. Cal's office was in the basement but it was like a separate apartment with its own bathroom and kitchen. I could hear Andrea moving around upstairs. She could hear me on the typewriter in the basement or see my truck in the driveway.

Yet, Andrea and I had something in common no one else had — Cal. That was never acknowledged openly between us. I did not want her to die without our meeting and talking.

I think I was wrong.

Forgive me but it is 2:30. I am going to bed.

Being open and honest with one's spouse is exhausting.

Friday, 9 A.M.

Bobby called at seven this morning, crying, pleading with me to help him with the arrangements for Andrea's funeral. I almost said yes. How do you refuse someone who needs you? And that's the lure that gets you into the trap.

I felt guilty for saying no to him. I feared saying yes, however, feared it would only be the first of many assents as Bobby desperately sought a replacement for Andrea and I am the only candidate because he and I shared the same beginning.

"Why don't you call Kathy? She and Adisa would love to help you, Bobby."

The suggestion startled him, but I think he might take it. He feels incapable of doing all that must be done to properly inter the widow of John Calvin Marshall. Bobby will have to make the decisions about who speaks at the funeral and who sits where and who sings what. He will have to say no to most and offend many for whom an appearance at Andrea's funeral is a major career move.

The funeral will be Monday. I will go only to the cemetery.

I am never convinced someone is dead until I see the casket put into the ground. When Jessica died, the funeral director didn't want me to stay for the lowering of the casket. I suppose that is the hardest moment for most survivors, the moment when you know, without a doubt, that there is now an emptiness in your life. If hysteria is going to be unleashed, I would imagine it is at that moment. So, he wanted me to go.

No one else was there. When Jessica died, there was no funeral. There was no one to say any words. There was only me. You offered to come but I didn't want you to. You would not have understood why my eyes were not only dry but glowing.

I told the funeral director I wasn't going anywhere until the burial was complete, and, in fact, if he could find an extra shovel, I would pitch in. I think it was then that he looked in my eyes and became afraid. I would not have been surprised if he had a momentary thought to call the police and to order an autopsy on the body to make sure she had died of natural causes.

But where is it written that we are to love our parents? Honor, yes. Love? How do you love someone when you had no say in creating the relationship? Love must be a choice. It was a choice Jessica and I did not make.

I did not love my mother, and for a simple reason. My mother did not love me. Generally, we love those who love us. Or, we think we do. You and me, for example.

I will go to the cemetery and see Andrea buried and that will be the end. And then, I don't know. Even though there's new snow at home, there's also snow in Colorado and New Mexico. I won't really know until I see her casket resting in the earth. Then, for the first time in my life, I think I will be free.

1 p.m.

I had not planned to write so much. My original thought had been to simply tell you what the silence at my core has been. That is proving to be harder than I thought. But I also find that I want you to understand, which is a surprise. But I owe you that. You have loved a woman who thought she loved you and found that she didn't but not because of you.

Do you remember a few years ago we were in the post office in Newport and I asked for some first-class stamps and the clerk gave me some with Cal's picture on it? They had just been issued. I shoved them back and asked for others. Afterwards, you said what I did seemed racist. I laughed and you were a little annoyed. And before that, the first year there was the national holiday named after Cal, you were angry that I wouldn't go to Burlington with you to attend a gathering at some church where I would have to listen to speeches by a whole lot of people who never knew him? You hinted again that my refusal "to honor the memory of John Calvin Marshall" made me a racist.

I can't tell you how sick I am of black people and their white sycophants shouting racism whenever they don't get their way. If there is anything more tyrannical than the tyranny of the oppressor, it is the tyranny of the oppressed and their fellow travelers.

Why didn't you ask me, Gregory, why I didn't want those stamps? Why didn't you ask me why I didn't want to "honor" Cal's memory by observing the holiday in his name?

Forgive me. I want it both ways, don't I? I berate you for wanting to understand me, for using the word, why, in my presence, and then I ask you to ask me why. What I really want is for you and me to live in such intimacy that you *know* when I need to be asked why and when I don't. How are you supposed to know the difference? What else is a husband supposed to know?

Gregory, the least that a husband and wife can expect is that they be kind to each other. Regardless of what else happens, kindness must prevail. If they can be kind even when they hate each other, the love will return as surely as a cat will when it runs and hides from the slamming of a door. But if there is no kindness, there is no ground for weary feet to stand on.

I have been unkind, Gregory, and I am sorry. Since the day we met I have chosen the silence of my own self-centeredness. Of course you have the right to ask why. Of course you have the right to seek to understand me. Understanding the ways of another helps us live with what would otherwise be unacceptable. I have made it impossible for you to understand. I have made it impossible for you to accept. (Being in Nashville, one tends to start thinking in Country and Western lyrics. I just thought of one that would describe what I've done to you: "Like a hound dog, I've kept you tied in the back yard of my life.")

"I envied you," Bobby said to me one night.

"Why?"

"Because you were with Cal more than anyone. God, I loved that man."

"Is that why you moved back here to work for Andrea?"

He shrugged. "I hadn't thought about it like that. I don't know. But I have a feeling you're trying to change the subject, or at least deflect it from yourself."

I had to smile. "There might be a measure of truth to that."

"I wish you would write a book about him. Nobody is more qualified. I read all the books about him and there is never any mention of you."

"Oh, they come with their tape recorders and notepads and smiles. Do they think I will tell them the truth merely because they want to know? And what makes them think they would recognize truth? What makes them think they have the capacity to understand and describe Cal?

"They ask their questions and I say nothing. They accuse me of withholding information. They remind me of my obligation to history, of what will be lost to posterity if what I know about John Calvin Marshall goes to the grave with me. I say nothing and eventually they leave. I read their books and I underline this and that and write angry rebuttals in the margins but I will not talk to them and I will not write my own book."

"I wanted Andrea to talk to you about her book. She responded rather cooly to the suggestion."

I have not told him why.

In the post office that day, I shoved the stamps back because I couldn't imagine licking a stamp on which was the image of the man whose penis I had licked for seven years. I saw Cal's picture on the stamp and immediately there came the image of his penis, long and thick and hard as a diamond. It was black, blacker than anything else on his body as if it had taken on the darkness of the inside of the vagina. The books say women don't care what size a man's penis is. That is because the only penises they have seen have been small. Believe me, it makes a difference. So, I'm looking at his likeness on a stamp and remembering his penis and my tongue and I try to imagine licking the gum on the back of the stamp but I see myself licking the semen as it flowed down the side of his penis, and, well, it was a little too much to deal with standing in the post office in Newport, Vermont.

Cal's penis was magnificent. If it had been a horse, it would have been a black Arabian stallion. If it had been a bird, it would have been an eagle. If it had been in the sea, it would have been a whale.

The penis is divine. Maybe not tiny ones like yours, but with Cal's I understood why, in India, lingams are set up at crossroads and women lavish them with lotion. The penis is divine because it is the instrument of life. Through it passes the seed of human existence. Through it, male and female are renewed spiritually. When sex is good, male and female arise from the bed with a new understanding of human existence. This new understanding never lasts long, however, which is why we want sex as often as possible. It is the means given to each and everyone of us to be more than we are.

Think about the penis, Gregory. What does it do? What is its function, really? It connects. Couple is a noun. It is also a verb. To couple is to make a connection whereby two who have been separate become one. That is what the penis does; it banishes loneliness, or it has that potential. Unfortunately, men are stupid. They think the penis penetrates. They think the penis is meant to thrust and jab and batter and so they bang and bluster and huff and puff until they have their orgasms, spill their seed and go to sleep, and then wonder why they harvest women's anger.

I am happy that Cal's last act in this life was using his penis. When the coroner stripped his body for the autopsy, his penis was still moist from the wetness of my vagina. Strands of semen hung from his penis like tiny ribbons.

I feel foolish telling you about his penis. But maybe, maybe if I share with you what I love, emotion will return color to the images and I will come back and live inside my body, even when I am not on skis.

I was a virgin when Cal and I first slept together. He was to be commencement speaker at my graduation. I was not surprised when the phone rang in my room at school late one evening about a week before commencement. I recognized his voice immediately.

"Elizabeth." No, "Hello." No, "How are you?" Just my name.

"Hi."

It was as if two years had not passed with no words between us. There was no chitchat. He gave me his flight number and I said I would meet him. I asked him what hotel he was staying at. He said he thought he was supposed to be staying at the president of the college's house, but he would prefer not to.

Cal was comfortable with me because I was not awed by him, not even then. Which is not to say that I don't think he was the most amazing man I've ever known or that I didn't admire him. I did and he needed that. But more, he needed someone who, at the most inappropriate moment, would whisper in his ear, "I am going to suck your dick so good tonight."

I know I never said that to you or did it. But a couple creates the modes of sexual expression appropriate for them. What would have sounded vulgar between you and me was exciting for me and Cal.

I didn't know if Cal wanted to see the press when he got off the plane. I thought not because he was flying out two days before he had to and had asked me to meet him at the airport. I called the airline, pretended I was a representative of the college and asked if it would be possible to drive onto the airfield and pick Cal up directly from the plane rather than have him come through the terminal? No problem. I asked Daddy if he could arrange for me to have a limo at Cal's disposal. And by the way, was anybody using his company's suite at the Ambassador Hotel? I called the college president's office, pretended to be Cal's secretary and told him that Dr. Marshall had a series of private meetings set up and would not be staying at the president's home.

I perceived needs Cal did not know he had and it gave me delight to satisfy them.

Love is simple, Gregory. There is nothing mysterious or difficult about it. Love is the taking delight in the existence of the other.

We never did that, did we? I don't know that you knew it was possible. But I did and I did not tell you.

It is just as well, perhaps, because I am not sure that any of what I've written about me and Cal is true. I am not sure that what I have written with such confidence was shared experience or imagined. I am not sure that my life, from the day I met Cal until this day has not been a fantasy, a deliberate lie because I was afraid the truth would shatter me.

Until ten days ago I had never spoken aloud one syllable about me and Cal. That's against the nature of love, isn't it? Love wants to be known. I was silent for thirty-two years about the central experience of my life.

I should have told you before we married. Maybe I was afraid you would call it off. No. I knew you wouldn't do that. I was more afraid you would be proud to be married to the mistress of John Calvin Marshall. No marriage stands a chance if it fears truth.

But what are the odds for a life that fears truth? Maybe Andrea was merely an excuse and it was time to stop lying. If you sit beside the bed of a comatose person and talk aloud for ten days, it becomes obvious quickly that it's yourself you need to talk to.

Like now. This moment. Am I talking to you, or am I continuing the conversation with myself? Am I using you to hear myself?

Perhaps it is both.

Speaking aloud is different than saying words to oneself. To speak aloud is to make the effort to couple with the other. What is important is to make the effort. Trying is its own success even if the loneliness is not bridged.

A few nights before Andrea died, Bobby and I sat in her house. It was a typical American ranch with a finished basement, which would have been the rec room if they had had children. I still had my key to the basement where Cal's private office had been.

Bobby wanted me to look at the manuscript, to tell him what I thought, and, I think, to feel me out about finishing it if Andrea should die.

There was scarcely anything to finish. Fifty pages of piety whose sweetness would have compelled readers to kick their children and shoot their dogs as the only means to restore a semblance of psychic balance.

There was no hint that John Calvin Marshall had had a relationship with another woman for most of his public career. According to Andrea, he was a devoted husband.

She might be right. The way she wrote of intimate conversations they had over coffee in the mornings and in the kitchen late at night, of phone calls when he would talk over problems and concerns he had about the civil rights movement, how to deal with presidents Kennedy and later Johnson, and his increasing agony over the Vietnam War.

I remembered clipping articles about the war and giving them to him from late sixty-two on. I read books and wrote precis for him. When Ngo Dinh Diem, the president of South Vietnam, was killed in a coup, I suggested to him that there might be CIA involvement. I was the one who first mentioned that one could not fight for civil rights at home and support a government depriving a nation in Southeast Asia of its right to choose its own destiny.

Why had he discussed all this with her and not me? I felt

betrayed, as if he had had an affair with his own wife. He wasn't supposed to be talking with her about matters he would not have known about if not for me. He wasn't supposed to be talking to her about anything that mattered to him, about anything that mattered at all.

He never told me about his conversations with Kennedy and Johnson. I have been trying to remember what we did talk about? I can't remember anything. Maybe that is why I am silent with his biographers. I have nothing to say. Maybe I talk so much about his penis because that is all I knew of him.

I try to convince myself that Andrea was lying, that she was creating a public fiction. For some reason I know she was not. Cal had to have a confidante, someone whom he could use as his sounding board. I was so self-centered that it never occurred to me that it would be his own wife. That's logical, right? That makes sense, doesn't it?

I feel so stupid.

Yet, his tears were not a lie. He may have shared his musings with her, but I was the one who lanced his pain and healed his soul.

I do not like myself very much at this moment. I read over what I have just written and I am ashamed. I am upset because I had fancied that I was the only one in the life of John Calvin Marshall and maybe I wasn't. Or maybe I was the only one in one part of his life and not another. Maybe he simply used me. Well, I was obviously anxious to be used.

No.

That is not how it was. Maybe what she wrote is true. Maybe it isn't. But lust cannot last seven years. No man sleeps with a woman for that many years from physical desire alone.

But at this moment, I am not sure.

Saturday — Evening

I have just returned from the cemetery. It is the first time I have seen where Cal is buried. Although it is not the setting I would have put him in, it is appropriate.

He is buried in a large cemetery near a shopping mall. His grave stone is a block of granite, and not having been here before, I was surprised by the words on his tombstone. "God's Gonna Trouble The Waters," they read. I would not have given Andrea credit for such insight. The words are from a spiritual called "Wade in the Water."

> Wade in the water
> Wade in the water, children
> Wade in the water
> God's gonna trouble the water.
>
> Who's that yonder all dressed in red?
> God's gonna trouble the water.
> It must be the children Moses led
> God's gonna trouble the water.
>
> Who's that yonder all dressed in white?
> God's gonna trouble the water.
> It must be the children of the Israelites
> God's gonna trouble the water.
>
> Who's that yonder all dressed in black?
> God's gonna trouble the water.
> Must be the hypocrites getting back
> God's gonna trouble the water.

At large mass meetings Cal would end his speech by breaking into that song. It was a familiar spiritual all across the South, and all he had to do was sing the first word and every black voice in the church would come in on the second. It would send chills through me every time because it was as if I was hearing not only their voices but the voices of their ancestors going back in time to that absurd moment white people made the decision that it was in their best interests to import dark-skinned people from halfway across the globe and enslave them. (And there are those who want to argue that white people aren't insane.)

I don't know that I ever understood the song as much as I loved it. What did it mean that God was going to trouble the water? Such a strange and unusual use of the word, trouble. Was it a corruption and was the line originally that God was going to tremble the water? It bothered me so much that I finally went to a library and looked it up and much to my surprise, I learned that there is a definition that means "To disturb, agitate, ruffle (water, air, etc.); esp. to stir up (water) so as to make it thick or muddy."

One night I asked Cal, "Why would God want to trouble the water?"

He looked at me sharply. "What do you mean?"

"That spiritual. God's gonna trouble the water. Why would God want to stir things up, to make them muddy? Why would God want to be an agitator, a disturber of stillness and peace?"

"Perhaps there are some waters that need disturbing."

I could tell that he hadn't thought about it himself, that he was trying to cover up that he didn't know and was too tired to really think about it at that moment.

A week later he was dead.

I hadn't thought about those words since and there they were on his tombstone. Well, his death had certainly troubled the waters. Had that been God's doing? If so, to what end? What did God benefit from troubled waters?

Next to his grave was the open earth where Andrea would

be laid. Do you remember my writing earlier that each death returns you to all your deaths? When I stared into Andrea's grave, it was also Jessica's and it was the grave of all those who died in the sixties, most of whom I knew only from the accounts I heard others give Cal, but I have made it a point all these years to remember their names and I recite them to myself at odd moments because everyone can't forget, Gregory. It isn't right that everyone go on with their lives as if they had not lived or died.

Rev. George Lee
Lamar Smith
Emmett Till
Willie Edwards, Jr.
Mack Charles Parker
Herbert Lee
Roman Ducksworth, Jr.
Paul Guihard
William Moore
Medgar Evers
Addie Mae Collins
Denise McNair
Carole Robertson
Cynthia Wesley
Virgil Ware
Louis Allen
Rev. Bruce Klunder
Henry Dee
Charles Moore
James Chaney
Andrew Goodman
Michael Schwerner
Col. Lemuel Penn
Jimmie Lee Jackson

AND ALL OUR WOUNDS FORGIVEN

Rev. James Reeb
Viola Liuzzo
Jonathan Daniels
Samuel Younge, Jr.
Vernon Dahmer
John Calvin Marshall

I have forgotten some names and I am sorry. And I don't know the names of all those like Bobby who are living but only barely, those who hemorrhage from wounds they don't know they carry, those who hurt and don't know it is from pains thirty years old.

I lay down on Cal's grave and it reminded me of all the times I had lain atop him after we made love. No, he did not tell me what he was thinking about the future of the civil rights movement or the Vietnam War or what Kennedy or Johnson had said because there was no space. There were other matters that needed saying.

We talked a lot about death. His.

I hated it. Every time he started I would want to shut him up, but, over time, I understood: he cared for me. I did not think about the difference in our ages. He did. He knew that he was the only thing of significance in my life and he worried about what would happen to me when he died. He would make me fantasize about what I would do — go to graduate school, start a surfing school, get involved in Daddy's business in which I was major stockholder. Marrying a dentist and living in Vermont was not one of the fantasies.

The night before he was killed he knew. We both did. It wasn't the kind of knowing that is in words; it was a knowing of the heart and the body. But to understand the death of John Calvin Marshall you have to understand what those last years were like.

One cannot live on intimate terms with his mortality for

too long without becoming mad or free. Most of us became mad. Some of us dramatically like Bobby. Most of us quietly. Cal became free.

Everyone knows he is going to die, but how many really believe it? Deep down, everyone thinks that everybody else will die except him. Our deepest secret is that we are the one who is going to live forever.

Those of us who worked in the civil rights movement could not have that illusion of immortality. Firefighters risk death but only when fighting a fire. Policemen risk death but only when on the job. The majority of policemen go through their entire careers and are never in a situation in which their lives are threatened. I cannot think of anyone in this century who lived in constant relationship to death like those of us who sought to make America whole and broke ourselves into pieces instead.

There was no escaping death. Death came suddenly. Was that car behind you just a car or was it following you? What about that car passing you? You learned to rely on your peripheral vision to catch any untoward move, or the hint of something pointing at you. When you stopped at an intersection you were aware of every car and every person on the street. Your eyes and mind were constantly finding escape routes, constantly plotting evasive maneuvers if a car came at you from this direction or that. You assumed death and so you never relaxed. The rifle which fired the bullet that killed William Moore belonged to a man Moore had had a friendly conversation with hours before. When the reality is death, you do not trust appearances.

That is something of what the daily reality was like for the average civil rights worker, someone working in a small town in Alabama or Mississippi. But that civil rights worker could go into the next county and there he was anonymous. That was why every six months or so, people who had been working in those small towns would pile into a couple of cars and go to New Orleans and party for an entire weekend. They had to remind themselves that joy existed and it was something for which they still had the capacity.

Imagine that you are John Calvin Marshall. Where do you go when you want to be reminded of joy? Where do you go to be out of the imaginary rifle-sight you know someone is always aiming at you in fantasy? The threat of death is constant. Death becomes your context for what is ordinary. If death is the ordinary, then where is life?

But this describes only one aspect of death with which John Calvin Marshall lived, and the least. Cal was fatalistic about assassination. When Kennedy was killed, he said, "If the Secret Service can't protect the president of the United States, what kind of protection do you think there can be for John Calvin Marshall?"

What almost drove him mad were the deaths of others. He felt responsible for each one, because their murderers had been impelled to action by the historical forces he had untied. He never permitted it to be publicized, but whenever there was a murder connected with the civil rights movement, he visited the survivors. Most of the time we went at night, just him and me in my pickup. No one ever knew. Sometimes it would be two or three in the morning when we would knock on the door of some shack in the middle of nothing. The family would not believe it was him. Sometimes we would not stay more than a half-hour. He would hug whomever the survivors were — the mother, father, wife, the children — and tell them how sorry he was.

The deaths and the grieving began to wear him down, especially after Shiloh. I don't know what happened there. All I remember is getting a call from him a little after midnight, Christmas morning. He told me to get Bobby out of the South as quickly as possible. I slipped on a pair of jeans and a shirt, jumped in my truck and left. When I got to Shiloh, it was Christmas morning, an overcast gray Christmas morning. I walked into the Freedom House. Bobby was seated on a sofa, staring into space as if he were incapable of speech and would never be again. George was sitting beside him.

I had seen him only occasionally since returning South. At staff meetings, primarily, and we never had the chance to talk. I'm not sure why.

"Bobby?"

He did not look at me or respond.

"What happened?" I asked George.

"If he wants you to know, he'll tell you."

I never liked George. He was the first black I ever met who didn't distinguish between those who were on his side and those who weren't. He hated white people and he hated me.

"What're you going to do?" he continued. "Cal send you?"

"If I want you to know, I'll tell you," I shot back.

I got on the phone and called someone who taught at a college in the midwest. I told him I was going to be leaving Shiloh within minutes. I had had two hours sleep and figured I could drive twelve hours without stopping to rest, which should put me close to him. He was to meet me and I would tell him what to do from there.

I hung up and made another call to a psychiatrist in New York who had started to treat some of our casualties. I told him I had a major one and he should expect me in the next twenty-four hours. He knew that if I were bringing someone personally, it was serious.

George helped me put Bobby in the truck. It was Christmas and I didn't think the highway patrol or state police would be on the roads to wonder about a white woman and black man in a truck.

I made it to Ohio and the person I'd called was waiting and together we drove nonstop to New York, deposited Bobby who looked as if he had never even blinked his eyes, drove back to Ohio and I went back to Nashville.

I went by to see Cal and told him where Bobby was.

He nodded his approval.

"You want to tell me what this was all about?"

He was silent for a long time. "No," he said finally. "I really really don't. It's a nightmare and I fear it is only going to get worse."

There was another long silence. "I've always known the dangers. I've always known that to awaken the Negro to take action against the evil stifling him would also mean rousing the Negro's own evil. Even before I embarked on the bus boycott in Atlanta in the late fifties, I worried about that. What would I do, what could be done when the centuries of anger extravasated?

"The stupidity of white America is terrifying. It does not require great intelligence to figure out that if you hate a people all you are doing is giving them lessons in how to hate you. And that's what Negroes have been learning all these years. Just because they haven't expressed it yet doesn't mean they haven't been taking notes and practicing in quiet.

"It was my hope that by creating a movement for social change I could circumvent the hatred. I was wrong. It is from within my very own movement the lava has begun to flow."

I understood his words but had no context. What had happened? Had Bobby done something awful? What was going on?

All he said was, "Thank you. You must trust me very much to do all you have just done and know so little."

"You know I trust you."

"I know. Your trust enables me to doubt and question and regret." He smiled weakly. "You are about to collapse. Go home and unplug your phone."

What Cal said that night didn't make sense until two years later at the famous staff meeting in the spring of sixty-six. Bobby was there, his eyes glittering with fever. He had been fund-raising in New York and had begun to acquire a following because of his impassioned rhetoric and a new-found ability to touch the guilt of whites in a way that made them write very large checks to assuage it.

Bobby had changed.

"He's gone mad," I told Cal.

"No. He is *suffering* the madness white America will not take responsibility for."

I was unprepared for the challenge to Cal's leadership from those who had gathered around Bobby. I was not prepared to hear Cal called an "Uncle Tom." I was especially unprepared when the motion was made that all whites in any way connected with the organization were to leave immediately.

I was sitting to Cal's right. I did not dare look at him but I had the feeling he was surprised too.

The motion was quickly seconded and the debate began.

The argument was simple: While there might have been a place for whites in the civil rights struggle, it was now a struggle for black liberation. The ideal of integration had failed because whites were not interested in living with blacks on an equal basis. The only alternative was for blacks to live with each other, to create the black economic, social and cultural institutions that would teach African values and sustain black men and black women.

I have never felt so dumb in my life. How could all of this

have been going on and me not notice? I knew nothing about black people. Absolutely nothing.

Then I remembered something. I looked through the folders I always had with me at staff meetings, found the document I was looking for, underlined a particular passage and handed it to Cal.

The debate went on for some time. Those who spoke against the motion did so weakly. It was apparent that the defenders of the motion had history on their side.

Finally, when it seemed everyone had had his say, Cal spoke. His voice was quiet, almost a whisper. "We must be careful that we do not become the evil we have been so intent on killing. We must be careful that our desire for justice is not so ardent that it becomes a thirst for vengeance. We must not only be careful; we must also take care. And taking care means pulling up the weeds that threaten to choke the fragile green new life breaking the earth. Taking care means watering that new life so it will not wither from lack of sustenance. Taking care means picking off the bugs that would eat the tiny leaves.

"The arguments put forth here are very appealing. If I were not careful I would be seduced by them. Who would not be? How simple it would be if we could create a world of blackness. How comforting it would be, and God knows, we need comfort. But this is not comfort. It is death."

His voice was stronger now but it was still not loud. He spoke conversationally and with deep sadness.

"It is obvious that my time is past. However, that does not mean I will hand over my organization to you or anybody. If you feel as you do, then be honest enough and men enough to go out and build your own organization instead of trying to take over the fruits of another man's labor. But, please understand. I will decide when I go. I, or a bullet. Nothing else.

"The motion on the floor is the expulsion of whites. The motion is out of order."

There was an outbreak of shouting and yelling. Cal waited until it died down.

"The motion is out of order because in Section 1, Paragraph 1 of our Constitution," and he picked up the sheet of paper I had underlined and slipped him when the debate began, "you will notice that it says, 'The Southern Committee for Racial Justice is founded on the principle of racial equality. Membership in the organization is open to people of all races, colors and creeds without restriction or qualification.'

"The motion is out of order. Next order of business."

Over the next few months three-quarters of the staff would leave to start a new group, Black Revolutionary Liberators. By this time, Bobby was in a hospital.

Without an effective organization any longer, Cal spent most of his time speaking on college campuses. The money was good and he had never had much of that. I went with him and I noticed that his audiences now were practically all white, but he never commented on it and neither did I.

Winter, 1969. I was the one who took the call in Cal's basement office. Gary Dunbar, one of Cal's oldest friends and a civil rights leader in Tackett, Georgia, had been shot and killed. Could Cal come?

It was the first time I had seen him want to say no.

Tackett was one of those little towns with only a general store and a post office to indicate there was an entity called a town. The place smelled of ancient deaths and unquiet ghosts. One would not have been surprised if the blue sky rained down blood.

We arrived early the next afternoon. Cal met briefly with the local leadership, and agreed to speak at a mass meeting that night and at his friend's funeral the next morning, but he refused to lead a march from the cemetery to the sheriff's office.

"Your march will be more effective if I am not involved."

"Our march will be more effective if we have somebody leading it who can get us some TV coverage," a young black kid said, glaring at Cal. "That's about all you're good for anymore. At least do that much."

Cal's head dropped to his chest. "I will not lead the march," he repeated.

But if there had been any doubt if people still wanted to hear John Calvin Marshall it was put to rest that night. The little church was filled, with people sitting in the windows and standing three deep outside.

I could not remember how many times I had heard him speak. From the first sentence I could tell which speech it was going to be. He had three basic ones and moved their various parts around to fit the situation.

That night though the beginning was unlike any I'd ever heard.

"The waters are troubled tonight. God has taken his servant, Death, and used him to agitate the placid stream. What was clear is now muddy. What was smooth is now roiled. What was placid is now disquieted.

"I came to bring peace and did not see the sword in its scabbard at my side. I did not see that it is not possible to correct injustice without committing it. I did not see that good is the creator of evil when good leaves evil unbefriended. I did not see and God has troubled the water.

"Oh, say, can you see?

"No, no, you can't. This afternoon when I came to town, some became angry with me because I would not lead them in a march to demand the sheriff find and arrest the murderer or murderers of Gary Dunbar.

"Oh, say, can you see?

"No, no, you can't. Can't you see that Gary's murder is not the author of your anger, and the prosecution of his murderers will not assuage your anger? Your anger makes you feel that, at long last, you have been blessed with righteousness, but righteousness humbles; *self-righteousness* emboldens.

"Oh, say, can you see?

"I see Ol' Death riding his white horse and he is taking a strange path. He is passing up the homes where the white folks live and is just stopping at those where black reside. But Death ain't no racist. Uh-uh. What does Death know that we don't? Death knows that white folks are already dead.

"Oh, say, can you see?

"Yes, they are. Only people who are passionately in love with Death build atom bombs and hydrogen bombs that can destroy the world many times over. Only people who are married to Death would spend more than half their national budget on weapons to kill. Only people who themselves want to be dead would think that accidents and killings are news to be put on the front page of papers and heard first on television. Only people who lust for Death would think skin color and hair texture and eye color could ever tell you anything about the quality of another human being.

"And now, black people are beginning their own love affair with Death.

"Oh, say, can you see?

"Black is beautiful! That's what they say. I'm black and I'm proud! Why? I want to ask. What effort did you put into becoming black? None. Then, why are you proud of it?

"Black is NOT beautiful. Don't you understand that if black is beautiful, then white has to be ugly, and doesn't that sound familiar?

"If I need to tell myself that I am black and proud, if I

need to tell myself how beautiful blackness is, am I not confessing my self-hatred? Am I not confessing how ugly I appear to myself?

"You are angry with the sheriff. No. You are angry at yourselves for having spent all your life as niggersniggers-niggers. Don't blame the white man. Just because he may want you to be a nigger doesn't mean you have to oblige him.

"Oh, say, can you see — nigger?"

I am glad I thought to set up the tape recorder because I would not have believed it if I could not have heard it again. I suppose I could give the tape to some biographer. No one knows it exists. There are rumors about a strange, incoherent speech he gave in Tackett the night before he died, but there has never been corroboration.

Most of the people left early. This was not the John Calvin Marshall they had heard about. They did not know who this crazy man was, and the nigger had to be crazy to drive into Tackett with a white woman, not to mention get up and say what he said.

But I understood.

John Calvin Marshall and Cal had become one. He was now free.

"You want to march to protest the killing of Gary Dunbar. Damn! That is not what Gary wants. He wants you to go out and do whatever it is he was doing that got him killed. You're angry! No angry person has ever been free!"

The church and the grounds were practically deserted when he finished, but Cal walked off the pulpit with a bounce in his step and a smile on his face.

He was approached by some of the men who had spoken with him that afternoon and I heard them say that they were sorry but they had to withdraw the invitation to speak at the funeral the next day. They were trying to get in touch with

Jesse Jackson and they might delay the funeral a day or two if Jackson could come.

We got in the truck and I asked him if he wanted to go home. He thought for a moment and shook his head.

"We have a free night. Let's make the best of it."

I saw the car pull in behind us when we drove out of Tackett. We were silent. The lights of the car following us were on bright and I put on my sunglasses. I did not dare speed to try to get away. It could have been the sheriff or the highway patrol, or one of them could have been waiting on a side road for us to come speeding by.

As we neared Atlanta and traffic became heavier the car lowered its beams and dropped back. I sighed deeply but was unaware of it until Cal asked, "Something wrong?"

"No. Why do you ask?"

"You sighed."

"I did?" I remembered. "Oh, the car that followed us from Tackett just lowered its beam and I guess I had been more concerned about it than I realized."

"How long have you been doing this?"

I thought. "Seven years."

"You sound tired."

Some of our most intimate moments were the nights we were going someplace in the truck. It was hard deciding whether it was more risky travelling at night or in the daytime. We preferred the night because he was a more difficult target and a following car was easier to see. I think he also preferred the night because the darkness intensified the stillness of the world around us until it seemed that no one existed except him and me in the dim glow of the dashboard lights. We seldom spoke. He would reach over, lift my dress or skirt and put his left hand between my thighs. I did not wear underpants then.

I have made love to only two men in fifty-two years. You

and Cal (and, Gregory, you may never read any of this. The gap between what I seem to need to say — everything in graphic detail — and what you may need to hear is increasing). And I have never *made* love with you.

That is no fault of yours. Nor mine. *Making* love requires a vision of who the two of you are, a vision as grand as any architect's for the ideal city but a city that will never be completed, regardless of how many structures are erected. We make the mistake of thinking that love is something that can be established once and for all, at which point, we marry and then work at maintaining what has been established.

That is one model, I suppose, but there is another. To *make* love daily by being attentive to the opportunities of transforming a mundane moment into a vehicle to express that the other matters.

His left hand would rest between my bare thighs, the heel against the mons veneris. I suspect other men would immediately institute the hunt for the orgasm. Not Cal. His hand would rest between my thighs, warm, and I would become aware of my thighs, my pubic hair, the labia majora. To *make* love is to awaken the beloved to her own being.

Cal said once that it was not his responsibility to make me have an orgasm. He only wanted to give me pleasure. He only wanted me to experience how beautiful I was. He only wanted to tell me — with his hands — how much I mattered to him. If he could do that, orgasms would come. Or they wouldn't.

"You haven't taken a day off in seven years," he continued.

"Neither have you," I countered.

"But you need a vacation more than I do," he said seriously.

I started to protest and he cut me off.

"When I got my doctorate and Andrea and I married, she expected that I would secure a position at some nice small college in one of those postcard New England towns and we would live happily ever after. I, however, assumed that she had felt at Radcliffe as I had at Harvard, which was like a sun without a sky to shine in. I couldn't wait to get back to the South. As lovely as Boston was, as much as I learned there, the bricks of the buildings and the bark on the trees did not connect me to a history that was mine. When I am in the South, I know who I am.

"I could not have done what you have. Seven years without an ocean wave. Seven years without strapping on skis. Seven years of living among a people not your own and I doubt that any of them has ever said thank you."

My hands gripped the wheel tightly and I didn't know if it was from wanting to deny what he had said or anger at its truth.

I drove to a hotel downtown. "Wait here," I said.

"What's up?" Cal wanted to know when I came back.

"*We're* taking a vacation. I just got us the penthouse suite. It has two bedrooms, each with kingsize bed and its own bath and a common living room big enough to house a family of eight easily. I explained to the manager that you would be occupying the suite and that you wanted privacy. I told her that I wanted one of their better bottles of red wine, two filet mignon tender enough to be mistaken for pudding, a hollandaise sauce delicate enough to feed a baby, asparagus tips, rice pilaf, a green salad with a lemon-mustard dressing, and we wouldn't need dessert because we would be eating each other."

He laughed.

As I turned into the hotel parking lot, the car behind me turned up its high beams, turned them down and continued along the street.

We knew but we did not acknowledge it in words to each other. And what would we have said? What words can express seven years of graceful intimacy? We were partners, two entirely separate beings creating a whole no other two people in either of our lives could have made.

A bellman met us in the parking lot. He was an old black man, a stereotype of the South with his ingratiating smile, eagerness to be of service, the shining blackness of his bald head.

I pointed to the bags in the bed of the truck. When we reached the penthouse I started to tip him and he refused.

"Ma'am, I carried the bag of Dr. John Calvin Marshall and saw him with my own two eyes. That's all the tip I need. God bless you, Dr."

The bellman had scarcely left when I answered a knock at the door and opened it to see the hotel manager standing there, flanked by two assistants, each holding a vase of flowers.

"Where would you like these?" she asked.

"I didn't order any flowers."

"Compliments of the hotel."

There was a vase of yellow and white roses, a vase of orange and red gladioli, and a vase of mixed wildflowers, zinnias, asters, and the like. The next knock was champagne, and an assortment of cheeses, crackers and dips.

God held back time that night. Each moment was as languid as a summer afternoon on a tropical island. We ate slowly and in silence.

He broke it once when he was holding the goblet of wine up to the light. "Look!" he exclaimed. "Look at the color! How extraordinarily beautiful. Look at the light sparkling off the redness of the wine!" He was like a child on Christmas morning looking at the Christmas tree. He lowered the goblet and sipped. "I suppose it isn't possible to do everything in one life, but I am sorry there was not more time for looking at the color of wine and the texture of hollandaise sauce."

When we finished I called room service, who came and removed the dirty dishes while Cal ran water for a hot bath. I was lying on the couch in the common room when I heard his voice.

"Elizabeth?"

I looked up. He stood in the doorway of the bedroom dressed in a thick wine-red bathrobe monogrammed with the hotel's initials. He beckoned for me to come. As I came abreast of him he took my hand and kissed me lightly on the lips.

He led me into the bathroom with its raised circular tub over the top of which the bubbles sparkled like light in wine. He unbuttoned my blouse, slowly, without hurried eagerness, slowly, as if there was no act more important in all the history of humankind, slowly, he slipped the blouse from my shoulder, down my arms and onto the tiled floor.

Lightly, his fingertips brushed my shoulders and down my arms. Deliberately he stayed away from touching my breasts, still covered by a black bra. There was wonder in his eyes as he stared at my torso and I wanted to know what he saw when he said, "I like the whiteness of you."

He unhooked my bra but did not remove it. Instead he took his index finger and moved it slowly from the tip of my chin, down my throat and chest, slowly, again and again, never touching my breasts as he passed them but slowing each time as if he were going to and then continuing past to my abdomen. I closed my eyes and there was no other meaning in the universe than the tip of his index finger barely touching my skin from throat to abdomen, over and over, patiently, as if he ruled time and held it in the palm of his hand.

Then, he added a second finger and I gasped as my body shivered involuntarily. Now as the two fingers moved down my torso, they came closer to the sides of my breasts, closer and closer. When a fingertip brushed the nipple of my left breast and then the right, I cried out and reached to pull him tightly to me, convinced that he would not be taken as long as my arms were around him.

He let me hold him for a moment as his fingertips now moved slowly up and down my back. Then, he moved back and gently removed the bra. We were still standing on the top of the platform next to the tub. I opened my eyes and saw him staring at my half-nakedness with the tenderness of a mother for a child. There was no lust or even desire in his gaze. There was only the passion of gratitude that I was and he was and that we had met and loved.

He unzipped my skirt, unholed the button on the side and slid it gently down my hips to the floor where I raised my feet for him to move it out of the way. He looked up at me, his eyes lingering at the mons veneris before continuing to my abdomen, my breasts, my face.

Finally, he stood and taking my hand, motioned for me to step into the tub. I expected him to follow, but instead he knelt beside the tub, pushed up the sleeves of the robe and taking a bar of soap, lathered his hands and began rubbing the suds across my shoulders, my back, my chest, his hands gradually sliding farther and farther down until he was fondling my breasts and I was spun into silk.

He had me stand and I felt I was being covered with a smooth body cream as his hands, lathered and relathered with soap, found my abdomen and then the firm globes of my buttocks, round and round and it was as if I had never been touched by those hands as if I had not known how beautiful I was to him and now a finger between the halves of my buttocks sliding easily into my anus while with his other hand he held the small oval of soap and moved it back and forth between the lips of my vagina, slowly, from the clitoris to the vaginal opening, pushing the end of the soap gently inside and then out, inside and out while the finger of his other hand slid in and out of my ass and I bent my knees in a modified skier's tuck so as not to lose my balance and my hips began moving back and forth in answer to his hands and as my thrusts became more definite and excited, his motions eased and rather than continuing toward a peak, he withdrew his fingers from my anus and vagina, and taking off his robe, stepped into the tub.

By now the water was tepid and he drained the tub until it was half-empty and pulling the shower curtain, turned on the shower to wash the lather from my body and when the tub was full again, I turned off the shower, took the bar of soap and began covering him with lather as thick as desire, but this was not the desire for sexual union as the desperate desire that he should live and not die, that this body which I knew so well, that this body whose every pore I had touched with my hands, my tongue, my breasts, that this body, which I had held close to mine night after night not begin its journey toward dust so soon, not while I had so much more love to lavish upon it upon his chest with its tiny nipples erect and hard beneath my fingernails and as his body leaned back against my breasts my nails dragged along his flesh from his abdomen up to his chest with ever increasing pressure, harder and harder and harder until he gasped with pain and the deeper my nails clawed, the slower I pulled them along his skin and he screamed and writhed, his body pushing backward into mine and I took a washcloth, rinsed off his neck and shoulders and with the quickness of a snake, my mouth and teeth grabbed the flesh of his neck and squeezed while my nails raked his body and his scream was not a loud explosion of noise but a thin high-pitched wailing like the sound of all the Africans captured on the winds of the ocean, a keening as the souls of all the African dead came from their graves on the floor of the Atlantic, from their unmarked tombs in the mud of Mississippi rivers coldwater sunflower tallahatchie pearl mississippi strong noxubee yockanookany homochitto Big Black yalobusha tombigbee from unquiet graves with lyncher's knotted ropes still hanging from their broken skeletons carrying the hard petrified remnants of their castrated members in their bony hands and he spun around and clung to me and his sobs reverberated with the hollow echoes of stone walls in the slave factories that had lined the coasts of Senegal Gambia Guinea sobs torn from lungs filled with ocean salt water when the sick were thrown over the sides of slave ships when the defiant leaped over sobbing sobbing sobbing the mothers and fathers of not only the slain the lost the forgotten but the sobbing of all those souls who would have been born from the slain the lost the forgotten if they had lived and his keening reached higher until it was barely audible but sustained and I heard him whisper "I am so sorry I am so sorry" but I did not know whose ears the words were for the fog was thick over the fields of shiloh that sunday morning new year's day morning as if this land which had seen more blood than anyone would ever know as if the land itself did not want to see anymore and wrapped itself in a winding sheet i had entered the fog within minutes after crossing from tennessee into missis- sippi and welcomed its protective secrecy enabling me to reach shiloh without anyone knowing i was in the state en- abling me to be alone and unseen and to think about what i would say and i knew it didn't matter whatever i said would not be heard at least not then at least not that morning but maybe the land would hear or maybe nothing would suffice except my life for theirs which i would not have called justice but was i not the one who had come to trouble the waters was i not the one who forgot it is not possible to evoke good without also evoking evil and evil begets evil with gleeful innocence in the souls of the young and idealistic and i did not know how to befriend evil i knew only that to treat evil as an adversary would only embolden it but what was the alternative it was a little past seven when i drove into shiloh and there was a young colored boy sitting beside the sign that said welcome to shiloh as if god had sent him there to wait for me and i asked him for directions to the house of jeb lincoln or sheriff simpson and he told me and i made my way through the fog to the lincoln plantation and the nondescript white farmhouse with the wraparound porch the yard was still and empty as i drove in and turned off the key i walked onto the porch but before i could knock the door opened and i faced a beautiful white woman with short dark hair, freckles and blue eyes she was holding a baby on one hip and i knew even less what to say because i had been expecting an older woman with the ample body of one who has borne her children and equally i supposed the woman holding the baby had not expected to open her door and see john calvin marshall and i knew she recognized me but i said anyway "i'm john calvin marshall" "even the dumbest nigger would know that" came the matter-of-fact response "i'm sarah lincoln, jeb's second wife his first one died of cancer this here is jeb the third" she stopped and looked at me with open and curious eyes as if despite the occasion she wasn't going to pass up the chance to see a celebrity to see if i looked just like i did on tv "never expected to see you standing on my porch" "who is it, sarah?" came the voice of a white man from inside the house "nothing to be concerned about" she yelled back and closed the door stepping onto the porch motioning me to follow her off the porch across the yard and to the other side of the barn where we would not be seen from the house "jeb has this thing about niggers like his pappy granpappy and their two pappys probably don't get me wrong or nothing i ain't got no brief for niggers and except for lucy the cook and thomas what clean up around the yard and do errands this is the closest i ever been to one of yall and i certainly don't agree with all the trouble you be stirring up niggers and white folks been getting along without no problem for a hundred years until you started stirring things up but jeb was never satisfied with just not liking niggers he had to let niggers know in the worst way that he didn't like 'em and who knows what he has done to niggers over the years it was a hobby like hunting and fishing and going to new orleans or memphis a couple of times a year to fuck black whores but it ain't like it used to be thirty forty years ago which is before my time but back then you could treat niggers however you wanted and wasn't nobody to say nothing about it but now if you look at one of them wrong john kennedy will send the fbi to your house and you'll be on the tv telling the niggers to rise up so i don't know why you come or what you want but it was a nervy thing to do and i guess just seeing you there when i opened the door was good enough for me i mean you ain't elvis or nobody like that but i ain't never seen nobody famous jeb never would take me up to nashville to see the grand ol' opry lots of famous folks there but ain't none of 'em famous as you and someday i might tell one of jeb's grandchildren that i met john calvin marshall it's a good thing i was coming down the steps when you knocked otherwise jeb might've answered the door and well you look like you're a good man john calvin marshall and thank you for coming" and walked me to my car and stood in the yard the baby perched on the shelf of her hip and she watched me drive into the fog and i didn't go to the sheriff's house and i didn't go see george stone but drove back to the highway north toward memphis and east to nashville and even though i had not told jeb lincoln or the sheriff that i was sorry that two people who worked for me had wanted to kill them i was glad i had gone because i was free now to grieve without guilt and I buried his head on my breasts and eagerly he took a nipple in his mouth and suckled, his arms tight around me as I cradled his head and rocked him.

Eventually he quieted. We noticed at about the same time that the water in the tub was cold. I opened the drain and we stepped out and dried each other with the large, fluffy towels. His penis was rigid and I took the head of it between the palms of my hands and rolled it back and forth and listening to his breathing get more and more shallow, I took his penis into my mouth and sucked on it hard as if I were trying to suck all the color from a popsicle without taking a breath and he came, his body twitching with spasms as scream after scream tore from his throat and I drank the thick semen hungrily.

We slept and I do not know for how long because neither of us was looking at clocks or watches but it was light when we awoke and he put his hand on my vagina and it was still wet and he pulled me atop him and I slipped his penis into me and so deeply was he inside me I wanted to ask him if he could feel the beating of my heart and because death was waiting impatiently now I came more quickly than I ever had and it was my turn to cry and be held and I felt so secure with his arms around me his penis inside me and me spread over him like a benediction.

When we finally dressed we were surprised to glance at the clock radio and see that it was one o'clock in the afternoon. I called down to the desk and told them we were checking out. I had signed the charge card slip the night before but the manager told me that everything would be taken care of by the hotel and a bellman would be up to get our bags.

When we got off the elevator in the lobby people were there with video cameras, which were new then, and still cameras. Ignoring them we followed the bellman to a side exit and to the parking lot.

"Dr. Marshall?"

The voice came from behind us. We turned and not until I saw the gun, saw the flash and heard the dull pop did I realize it was happening. I never saw the man, just the gun, the flash, the dull pop, and Cal fell against me and I caught him and we went down. As we did a second bullet passed where I had been and, not finding me, struck the old bellman whose grandchildren would not remember him as the man who had carried the bags and shook the hand of John Calvin Marshall but as the man who died with him.

Cal lay across my lap and I gathered him in my arms and held him against my breasts and I could feel his warm blood, his life, leaking onto my clothes. I thought he was dead already but his eyes opened and we stared at each other and he pulled me near and whispered in my ear. My heart froze.

Then he tried to raise his arm and I took his hand and placed it inside my blouse against my breast

and he died.

the voice was a nasal one and i could hear the evil in it as it spoke my name and i thought "now?" not in surprise or protest as much as wanting to recognize the moment and i turned and i saw a small balding head atop a pudgy body he wore wire rim glasses and his face was beatifically calm and i tried to reconcile the evil i heard in the way he called my name and the peace on his face but there was not time and spark of detonation sound of propulsion and meeting of steel and flesh were almost simultaneous and the bullet plunged into my chest and i thought i saw the gun in his outstretched hands move to the left and take aim at elizabeth and i fell against her pushing her to the ground for an instant it was dark and i wondered if this were death and then i felt her arms around me her breasts against my face and i opened my eyes and i could feel the frantic fluttering of my heart as it struggled to maintain its life knowing it could not and i hoped that she would understand and she would trust and she would know the need and i opened my mouth and she leaned over to hear me whisper "tell andrea i never stopped loving her" and i looked into elizabeth's face again and saw that she did not understand and i wanted to say and could not and i tried to raise my hand to place behind her head and draw her lips onto mine but she took it and placed it inside her blouse against her bare skin and onto her naked breast and she understood and

I still have the dress.

x.

we met once, two months before he was killed. he spoke at fisk and afterwards came to the house to see me. this was after his break with the nation of islam. he was reaching out, seeking allies among those of us he had just months before called "uncle toms" and "handkerchief heads" and "house niggers." i wanted to ask him how many times he had been beaten, how many nights he had spent in southern jail cells, how many times he had stared at death.

he was tall, taller than i expected, and earnest. his sincerity was unleavened by doubts or questions or musings. he *knew* the truth. that frightened me.

we did not have much to say to each other. he said that despite our differences, we had the same goals — the freedom of our people. i wanted to ask him what freedom was. i was not sure i knew anymore. i was not sure that freedom was a condition that could be attained by an entire people but only by isolated and very solitary individuals who had submitted.

he did most of the talking. i doubt that had been his intent, but i sensed he was nervous. people often were when they met me. perhaps it was the disparity between what i looked like physically and what i had done. our culture has its images of courage as it does of beauty and courage dresses in biceps. i had none. yet, in their minds were the pictures of me being beaten at the bus station in birmingham, me standing before the quarter of a million that august day in washington, me leading a march along mississippi highways.

x talked about our mutual love for our people. he acknowledged the risks i had taken, the sacrifices i had made, but he never apologized for all the times he had derided and mocked me and called me odious names, implying that i was a traitor to the very people he now claimed we both loved.

i said nothing, and after a while his words sputtered to a period and there was silence. he looked at me expectantly. i looked at him, the close-cropped hair, the dark necktie, white shirt and suit.

he did not like the silence and he sputtered back into language, telling me just how much i was doing for the cause of black identity. it was then i understood that i was confronting the future. he was seeking his identity and thought it could be found in the public arena. he was on a personal quest for salvation.

"i love white people, too," i interrupted him.

he was startled. "i beg your pardon."

"you said we both loved black people. i love white people, too. whatever i have done has been for them, too."

"but white people don't love *you,* my brother."

"and why do you think love must be reciprocated to be love?"

he laughed nervously. "this is getting a little philosophical for me." he stood up and extended his hand. I stood up and grasped his and we were aware that we had nothing more to say to each other — ever. and i think he knew that, if necessary, i would speak out against him with all the power and influence i could muster. not that it would do any good. history is as likely to side with those who are mistaken as the rest of us.

it does not surprise me that it is he who is loved and re-membered now. i have a holiday and a stamp but i am not loved. i am not missed. the changes for which i was the catalyst are dismissed as unimportant or taken for granted. and he who wrought no changes is enshrined in the hearts of a new generation.

lyndon would understand.

even though he never called me after i spoke out against the vietnam war, we understand this about the other: we had a vision of what america could be and it was not a vision of white against black and black against white. it was an ethic which had at its center a hatred of suffering.

few care about suffering anymore. they merely want to prove themselves right and everyone else wrong.

if only we knew how wrong we all are.

ANDREA

When the moment came, it was almost too late. She did not want to open her eyes because she was afraid they would not shut again, and what she wanted most of all now was that peace awaiting her behind the closed lids. But she had to open her eyes so Lisa would know that she had heard and in the hearing was the atonement and in the atonement was her humanity.

Lisa had been talking, but Andrea could no longer concentrate on the words, heard not meaning but only sound like a solitary chant on the other side of a hill, and that was enough now. The words did not matter. Only the chant.

Slowly, she forced the lids apart. Her gaze was met by a pair of startled blue eyes and Andrea's eyes filled with tears as she looked at the white woman and she wished she could say and say and she hoped Lisa understood but she did not want to keep her eyes open anymore could not stay here any longer and the lids came together — for the last time.

ROBERT

As Robert drove into the cemetery that Saturday afternoon he was not surprised to see, in the distance, the figure of Lisa lying atop Cal's grave. He had gone by the Holiday Inn and not finding her, did not know where else she would be.

He would have come here in any event — to see the dug grave and scratch from his list one more item he would not have to worry about. Kathy and Adisa were taking care of hotel reservations for those staying over, arranging catering for the reception after the funeral. He parked the car some distance from the graves that were his destination, not wanting to startle Lisa by entering her silence too abruptly.

Although it was late afternoon, and the sun was dropping quickly, there was a warmth in the air still. For reasons that were not at all clear, Robert felt young. He wanted to add "again" but couldn't remember when he had ever felt young. This sense of youthfulness was not coltish, however. If anything he felt more stolid than ever and in command, and that was something he had never experienced. Perhaps authentic youth was earned and came when one had survived the worst and knew he could survive even worse. Not only was there no more self-doubt about the quality of who he was, neither were there recriminations for all he was not.

As he walked toward the gravesites of John Calvin Marshall and Andrea Williams Marshall, he looked idly at the names on tombstones and tried to imagine a day when some-

one would walk through a cemetery and read his name —
Robert Charles Card. Would there be a Saturday afternoon
when Amy would lie atop his grave and make love to him
even in death?

He doubted it.

("Oh, God, no! Oh, God, no! I'm so sorry! I am so sorry
for you," she exclaimed that morning on West End Avenue.

He had expected she would take him in her arms, had
expected her to say something about how awful he must be
feeling and was he all right and what could she do, but she
was silent.

He looked at her. Her eyes were clear, expressing an ob-
jective concern, the kind she would have shown for anyone
who had just heard of the death of a friend.

Finally, she smiled sadly. "I'm very sorry, but I'm tired of
your emotions. I'm emotionally worn out. I have nothing
more to give you and my capacity to receive your pain has
been exhausted."

"You don't understand. You don't know what it was like."

"No, I don't. I don't know what it is like for someone in
the jungles of Vietnam who screams out in his sleep. I don't
know what it was like for someone in the jungles of Mississippi. All I know is that I tried to make it better and I ended
up feeling worse. There comes a time, Bobby, when you
have to take responsibility for your own pain, regardless of
who inflicted it on you. It seems like a lot of blacks in America are trying to avoid that truth these days and think that
if they blame white people long enough and loudly enough,
they will be healed. We tried that, Bobby."

"Fuck you, bitch!"

She laughed. "Not anymore. You can't fuck me or fuck
me over. Amy! You just might be growing up, girl. You just
might!" She waved good-bye and as the light changed yellow,
ran across the avenue and continued toward Broadway.)

He was closer now and could see Lisa lying with her eyes closed, cheek pressed to the earth over Cal's grave. For an instant, Robert was saddened that so much love and so much devotion was not being given to someone living, and for once, he did not think of himself.

But who was he to say that the dead did not need love, also. And maybe a special kind of love was required for the dead, a love that did not need love in return, a love whose reward was in loving.

As he moved closer, she felt the tremor of his weight upon the earth, opened her eyes and raised her head. When she saw who it was, she sat up and rested her back against the massive headstone marking the resting place of John Calvin Marshall.

"I hoped I would find you here," he greeted her, sitting in the grass at the edge of the grave. "Kathy told me you had called and said you were leaving. I stopped by the Holiday Inn and you weren't there. I couldn't think of any other place you would be."

"I could've been in Centennial Park."

"I beg your pardon?"

"Centennial Park."

"I know where Centennial Park is. Why would you go there?"

"Because I'd never been."

"All the years you lived in Nashville, you never went to Centennial Park?"

"Uh-uh. It was segregated. Remember?"

"Sure, but it was desegregated a year or two after the sit-ins."

"I know, Bobby. I know. But I've been angry all these years because it *had been* segregated, and I hated it that people acted like nothing had ever happened. Well, this afternoon I went and sat on the steps of the Parthenon and felt so foolish. It was nice sitting there in the afternoon sun and I thought about all the afternoons I could have sat there and felt the sun and didn't."

He nodded. "I know what you mean. Maybe that has something to do with why I wanted to see you before you left. I wanted to thank you."

"For what?"

"For telling me to call Kathy and Adisa."

"It worked out all right?"

"I could've been sitting on the steps of the temple and soaking up the sun for the past twenty years."

"Well, maybe it's not important when you sit on the steps but that you do."

She smiled. There was now an ease between them, an ease available only to those who have accepted that they are simultaneously less than they ever thought they were and more than they can ever know.

"You and Cal were lovers," he said simply.

She nodded.

He laughed softly. "I never knew until a few minutes ago when I saw how you lay atop his grave."

"The only one who knew for sure was Andrea."

He chuckled. "Now I understand why she didn't want to talk to you about her book."

"Well, if she had lived, it would be a different book now."

"How so?"

"I talked to her. I told her about me and Cal. I tried to get her to understand."

"I talked to her, too, after you gave me the idea. I told her things I had never said aloud to anyone. I don't think I could've done it if I had really believed she was listening."

"She knew that."

"What do you mean?"

"I'm not sure. All I know is that right before she died,

she opened her eyes and looked at me and her gaze was clear and alert and so alive. She didn't look like someone who had been in a coma for ten days."

"She heard everything we told her?" he asked, not sure if he liked that.

Lisa nodded. "I think she heard a lot more than we knew. And I'm glad. I'm glad she didn't die without hearing what I came to tell her."

"May I ask what that was?"

She thought for a moment. "Cal's last words were, 'Tell Andrea that I always loved her.' "

There was a long silence before she continued. "I'm sorry it took me so long to tell her. But I can't tell you how much it hurt me that his last words were giving me instructions to convey his love to his wife."

"Maybe he loved you so much he could entrust you with even that."

She nodded. "I think I understand that, finally. When I told her, her eyes opened and I was so startled and frightened I couldn't move or look away and we just stared at each other. I think she was trying to thank me. A tear formed in one eye, spilled over and trickled down her face. I took her hand and held it tightly. Her eyes closed and she was dead.

"I sat with her for a few minutes, wondering if she had kept herself alive until she heard what she needed to hear. And then I noticed that I was feeling happy."

"Me, too! Ever since she died I've been feeling like I didn't get the chance to feel when I was sixteen."

"Yes, yes. I think for me the feeling came when I told her Cal's words. That was Cal's final gift to me. I wonder if he had told me to do it not only because she needed to hear it but because I needed to say it. I would be free only when all of his truth meant as much to me as my own truth. Part of his truth was that he loved her."

"So, what are you going to do?"

"I don't know. I've been writing a long letter to my husband, but I don't know if he'll ever get to read it. I need to say something to him but I think what I wrote was what I needed to say to me. I'll probably go home and catch the last snows of the winter and then, I'll see."

"I've got to go," Robert said, standing up. "There're still a thousand details to tend to for the funeral."

She got up. "Let me give you a hug. You take care of yourself, and Kathy and Adisa. Marry her, Robert."

They held each other tightly for a long moment, then separated.

"I'm glad you were here," he told her. "Then and now."

"Thank you." She gave him another hug and he turned and walked away.

When he got to his car he looked back.

Elizabeth lay atop the grave like an answered prayer.